"Wait!" I said suddenly, dropping the card.

"What's the matter?" Dad asked.

"I forgot something."

I ran up to my room and grabbed a new pack of baseball cards from my desk drawer.

"They have bathrooms in 1932, y'know," Dad joked when I got back.

"I didn't go to the bathroom," I explained. "A baseball card is like a plane ticket for me. The Ruth card will send us to 1932. But it won't get us back *home*. We need to bring a *new* card with us for that. If I didn't have one with me, we would have been stuck in 1932 forever."

"Is there anything else you forgot?" Dad asked, a little annoyed.

"No, let's do it."

Other Books by **Dan Gutman**

HONUS & ME
JACKIE & ME
SHOELESS JOE & ME
JOHNNY HANGTIME

BABE
& Me

A Baseball Card Adventure

Dan Gutman

■ HarperTrophy®
An Imprint of HarperCollinsPublishers

Harper Trophy® is a registered trademark of
HarperCollins Publishers Inc.

Babe & Me
Copyright © 2000 by Dan Gutman

Library of Congress Cataloging-in-Publication Data
Gutman, Dan.
Babe & me : a baseball card adventure / by Dan Gutman
p.   cm.
Summary: With their ability to travel through time using vintage
baseball cards, Joe and his father have the opportunity to find out
whether Babe Ruth really did call his shot when he hit that home run
in the third game of the 1932 World Series against the Chicago Cubs.
ISBN 0-380-97739-7 — ISBN 0-380-80504-9 (pbk.)
1. Ruth, Babe, 1895–1948—Juvenile fiction. [1. Ruth, Babe,
1895–1948—Fiction. 2. Baseball—Fiction. 3. Time travel—Fiction.
4. Fathers and sons—Fiction.] I. Title. II. Title: Babe and me.
PZ7.G9846Baf 2000   99-36778
[Fic]—dc21   CIP

First Harper Trophy edition, 2002

**Dedicated to the *real* heroes—
teachers and librarians**

Acknowledgments

Thanks to SABR—the Society for American Baseball Research—and, in particular, Morris Eckhouse, John Zajc, Bob Bluthardt, Bill Carle, Rich Topp, and Neal Poloncarz. Also, I appreciate the help I received from Kirk Kandle, Mary Brace, Barbara Perry, Pete Williams, Paul Dickson, Nina Wallace; from David Kelly at the Library of Congress; from Elise Howard at Avon Books; from Greg Schwalenberg at The Babe Ruth Birthplace and Baseball Center; from Bill Burdick at the National Baseball Hall of Fame; from Mark Renvitch at the Franklin D. Roosevelt Library; from Joan Carroll at Associated Press/Wide World Photos; and from Tony Conte of Conte's Card Castle in Haddonfield, New Jersey.

BABE

& Me

The Mystery

IT'S THE GREATEST MYSTERY IN THE HISTORY OF SPORTS. It's *one* of the greatest mysteries of the twentieth century.

And I was the only person in the world who could solve it.

These are the facts:

The date: October 1, 1932

The place: Wrigley Field, Chicago, Illinois

The situation: The Chicago Cubs and New York Yankees played Game Three of the World Series on this day. In the fifth inning, Babe Ruth belted a long home run to straightaway centerfield.

This is the mystery: Did the Babe "call his shot"? Or not?

According to legend, just before he hit that homer,

Babe pointed to the centerfield bleachers and boldly predicted he would slam the next pitch there.

I've played a lot of baseball. Maybe you have, too. Hitting a baseball is not easy. Hitting a baseball to one side of the field or the other *on purpose* is very hard. And saying you're going to hit a home run on a specific pitch and to a specific part of the ballpark with the pressure on, well, that's just impossible. A batter who calls a shot like that is either incredibly lucky, crazy, stupid, or gifted. Maybe all four.

The closest witnesses to Babe's called shot—the Cub and Yankee players—disagreed. Some said Babe called his shot; others said he was only pointing and yelling at the Cub pitcher, Charlie Root. Some said the whole story is a myth that the press dreamed up to glorify Babe Ruth.

A few years ago somebody found a fuzzy home movie of Ruth at the plate at that moment. He

A few years ago somebody found a fuzzy home movie of Ruth at the plate at that moment.

pointed all right, but it's impossible to tell exactly *where* he was pointing.

People said it didn't matter if Babe called his shot or not. All that mattered is that he hit the home run.

Well, it mattered to *me*. I wanted to know the truth.

There was only one way for a human being to solve this mystery—to travel back to October 1, 1932, and see what happened.

The amazing thing is, I could *do* it.

Joe Stoshack

1

The Tingling Sensation

IT WAS ABOUT EIGHT YEARS AGO—WHEN I WAS FIVE—
that I discovered baseball cards were sort of . . .
oh, magical to me.

It was past my bedtime, I remember. I was sitting at the kitchen table with my dad. This was
before my mom and dad split up, before things got
weird around the house. Dad was showing me his
collection of baseball cards. He had hundreds, a few
of them dating back to the 1920s.

My dad never made a lot of money working as a
machine operator here in Louisville, Kentucky. I
think he spent all his extra money on his two pas-
sions in life—fixing up old cars and buying up old
baseball cards. Dad loved his cars and cards. They
were two of the things Dad and Mom argued about.

Anyway, we were sitting there at the table and
Dad handed me an old card.

4

"That's a Gil McDougald card from 1954," Dad said. "He was my hero growing up. What a sweet swing he had."

I examined the card. As I held it in my right hand, I felt a strange tingling sensation in my fingertips. It didn't hurt. It was pleasant. It felt a little bit like when you brush your fingers lightly against a TV screen when it's on.

I felt vibrations. It was a little frightening. I mean, it was only a piece of cardboard, but it felt so *powerful*.

"Joe," my dad said, waving his hand in front of my face, "are you okay?"

I dropped the card on the table. The tingling sensation stopped immediately.

"Uh, yeah," I said uncertainly as I snapped out of it. "Why?"

"You looked like you were in a trance or something," Dad explained, "like you weren't all there."

"I *felt* like I wasn't all there."

"He's overtired," my mom said, a little irritated. "Will you stop fooling with those cards and let Joey go to bed?"

But I wasn't overtired. I didn't know it at the time, but a baseball card—for me—could function like a time machine. That tingling sensation was the signal that my body was about to leave the present and travel back through time to the year on the card. If I had held the card a few seconds longer, I would have gone back to 1954 and landed somewhere near Gil McDougald.

After that night I touched other baseball cards from time to time. Sometimes I felt the tingling sensation. Other times I felt nothing.

Whenever I felt the tingling sensation I dropped the card. I was afraid. I could tell something strange was going to happen if I held on to the card. I didn't know what would happen, and I wasn't sure I wanted to find out.

Gradually, I discovered that the year of the card determined whether or not it would cause the tingling sensation. Brand-new cards didn't do anything. Cards from the 1960s to the 1990s didn't do much. But I could get a definite buzz from any card from the 1950s. The older the card, I discovered, the more powerful the tingling sensation.

One day, I got hold of a 1909 T-206 Honus Wagner card—the most valuable baseball card in the world. The tingling sensation started the instant I picked up the card. It was more powerful than it had been with any other card. For the first time, I didn't drop the card.

As I held the Wagner card, the tingling sensation moved up my fingers and through my arms, and washed over my entire body. As I thought about the year 1909, the environment around me faded away and was replaced by a different environment. It took about five seconds. In those five seconds, I traveled back through time to the year 1909.

What happened to me in 1909 is a long story, and I almost didn't make it back. After that, I didn't think I would ever travel through time with a baseball card again. But once you discover you've got a special power, it's hard not to use it. For a school project, I borrowed a Jackie Robinson card from a baseball card dealer and sent myself back to the year 1947.

I nearly got killed in 1947, and my mom grounded me. She didn't make me stay in my room or anything like that, but she did make me stay in the present day.

"No more time traveling!" she ordered.

But, like I said, when you've got a special power, you want to use it.

2

Use Your Head

"SMASH IT, STOSHACK!" ONE OF MY TEAMMATES YELLED as I pulled on my batting glove. "Hit one outta here so we can *get* outta here."

I snorted. Nobody has *ever* hit a ball out of Dunn Field, the park where most Louisville Little League games are played. It's not because the outfield wall is so deep. It's because it's so *high*. The plywood fence in left-, center-, and rightfield extends twenty or thirty feet off the ground.

The wall is plastered with ads for just about every hardware store, car dealership, dry cleaner, and supermarket in Louisville. The Little League sold a lot of ads this year, so they made the fences even higher to have a place to put them all.

Casey Tyler—one of the kids on my team—hit a ball off the wall once. In left center. He only got a double out of it because the ball bounced right to the centerfielder. I hit pretty good—I mean, pretty *well*—but I can't imagine hitting one out of Dunn Field.

"Be aggressive, Joey," Coach Zippel hollered, cupping his hands around his mouth. "That baseball is your worst enemy! Slam it."

My team, the Yellow Jackets, was down by two runs. There were two outs in the bottom of the sixth inning, which is all we play in the league for thirteen-year-olds. As I stepped into the batter's box, Casey Tyler took a lead off second base and Kevin Dougrey edged off third.

"Run on anything!" Coach Zippel yelled. "Two outs."

I pumped my bat back and forth a few times. The pitcher wasn't so tough. I had already singled off him. A solid hit would score both our runners and tie the game. An out of any kind would end the game, with our team losing.

"Smack one, Joey!" my mom shouted. She was sitting in the "mom" section of the bleachers. That's where all the moms sit. I don't think any of them are big baseball fans, but they like to get together and gossip and stuff while we play.

The dads are usually around the field, shouting encouragement and advice to us. Most of the dads show up for our games if they can. Even though he loves baseball, my dad has never been to one of my games. He says he can't get off from work, but I think it's really because he doesn't want to see my mom unless he has to.

In fact, we live only 250 miles from St. Louis, but my dad has never even taken me to a Cardinals game—or any big-league game.

As I dug a cleat into the dirt, I snuck a peek at the fielders. I bat lefty, so the defense had shifted to the right a little.

The third baseman, I noticed, was playing almost right on the foul line and way back—just behind the third-base bag. He wanted to keep Kevin close to the base, I knew, and he wanted to prevent a double or triple down the line.

A thought flashed through my brain: I could drop a bunt in front of that guy and beat it out. Kevin would score from third easily and Casey would advance to third. It would take everybody by surprise.

I didn't want to talk my idea over with Coach Zippel. If the other team saw me go over to him, they might suspect something was up. Besides, there was no time. The pitcher was going into his windup.

I waited until the last possible instant to square around and slide my hand up the barrel of the bat.

"He's layin' one down!" the coach of the other team screamed.

The pitch was right over the plate, just where I like it. I held the bat out the way Coach Zippel taught us in our bunting drills. You're supposed to sort of "catch" the ball with the bat. The idea is to tap it just hard enough so the catcher can't pounce on it, but softly enough so it stops far in front of the third baseman. It was a good bunt, I thought.

When the ball hit the bat, I broke for first. The third baseman made a dash toward the plate as soon as he saw me squaring around to bunt.

From the corner of my eye, I saw him reach down and scoop up the rolling ball bare-handed. In one motion, he whipped it underhanded toward first. He made a great play, but I thought I had it beat. As my foot hit the first-base bag, I heard the ball pop into the first baseman's mitt.

"Out!" bellowed the umpire. "That's the ball game!"

"What?" I yelled, turning around to find the ump. "I beat it out! I beat the ball to the bag!"

"Son, I had the best seat in the house," the ump said, "and you were out."

"Oh, man!"

The kids on the other team were pounding the third baseman on his back and congratulating him on his great play. My teammates just packed up their gear. Nobody gave me a hard time about it, but when I got back to the bench, Coach Zippel pulled me aside.

"Why'd you bunt, Joey?" he asked, his arm on my shoulder. I could tell he was angry, but he was doing his best not to show it. The coaches in our league are supposed to encourage us, even when we mess up.

"I saw the third baseman playing way back," I

explained. "I thought I could drop a bunt in front of him."

"But, Joey, you're a good hitter. You could have tied the game for us with a hit. Even if you had been safe at first on the bunt, we only would have scored one run. We needed two. And Frankie was up next."

Frankie Maloney was our worst hitter. The coach didn't come out and say it, but we both knew there was no way Frankie would have driven in the tying run. That was *my* job. I messed up.

"I hadn't thought of that," I admitted. "I'm sorry, Coach."

"Don't be so afraid to take a big old rip at the ball, Joey," the coach advised me. "If you would only let loose, there's no telling how hard you might hit it."

All the way home from the game, I sulked. The coach was right. I was too cautious. I *wanted* to hit the ball hard, but when the pressure was on and the pitch was coming in, something stopped me. So I usually took a halfhearted swing. Or I thought up some excuse to bunt.

"It was a beautiful bunt, honey," Mom said, trying to cheer me up as we pulled into our driveway. "You did the best you could."

Mom doesn't understand baseball. Everybody makes an error from time to time, but there's no excuse for a guy to make a dumb decision like I did. I never should have bunted. I should have swung away. Mom just saw the play, not the strategy.

My mom is Irish and my dad is Polish. Not that it matters or anything, but I thought you should know a little about me. Mom is a nurse at the University of Louisville Hospital. I don't have any brothers or sisters, though I guess I would have if my folks had stayed together. I've got a couple of cousins, but they live in Massachusetts and we hardly ever get together.

"Your father is coming over after dinner," Mom said as she cleaned a carrot for dinner. "He says he has something he needs to talk to both of us about."

"What is it?"

"He wouldn't tell me," Mom said, digging into the carrot a little harder than was necessary.

I don't know why my parents got divorced. I'm not sure if my mom or dad knows, either. One time I asked my mom about it, and she said my dad was angry all the time. He would never say what was really bothering him. Like it was some big secret or something. For years Mom tried to get him to talk about what troubled him, but finally she decided she just couldn't live with him anymore.

Dad lives in an apartment across town. He comes over to see me from time to time, but I don't feel all that comfortable with him. I guess I blame him for divorcing Mom, even if it was her idea.

"How'd you do in your game today, Butch?" Dad asked when I opened the door. He's always called me Butch.

I felt like telling him he could have seen for

himself how I did, if he had only come to the game. But I didn't want to set him off.

"I did okay," I said unenthusiastically. "Got a hit."

"That's my boy."

"What did you want to talk to us about, Bill?" Mom asked. She never liked to chitchat with Dad.

Dad shuffled his feet a little and looked down uncomfortably, a sure sign of bad news.

"I got laid off again," he said finally. "Business is slow. They had to get rid of people. Naturally, I was the first to go. I got no luck."

"You'll get another job, Bill," Mom said.

"Yeah? What do you know? Who's gonna hire me?"

Dad's eyes flashed anger. It was like he was blaming Mom for losing his job, when all she was trying to do was comfort him.

"The newspaper is filled with ads for guys who do what you do," Mom tried again.

"Sure, if I want a crummy job that pays nothin'."

Mom sighed. When Dad got into one of these moods, there was nothing anyone could say or do that would make him cheer up. Wearily, Mom took out her checkbook and started writing.

"I didn't come here to ask for more money, Terry."

"Just take it," Mom said, handing him a check.

He ripped the check in half and handed it back to her.

"Joe," Dad said, turning to me, "do you still have that old Babe Ruth card I gave you a while ago?"

"Sure, Dad."

"Would you be really upset if I asked for it back?"

It must have been really tough for him to ask that. He gave me the Ruth card as a present when I turned twelve. He must be selling off his card collection, I figured. He must need money pretty badly.

"Don't ask Joey to return a gift," Mom lectured him. "I'll lend you money."

"Quiet, Terry."

"I'll get the card," I said.

I keep my older, more valuable cards in clear plastic holders. This is partly to protect them and partly because I get that tingling sensation when I touch them. I wouldn't want to send myself back through time accidentally.

The Ruth card was the gem of my collection. It was from 1932 and very rare. My dad got the card for next to nothing from some lady who'd sold her husband's old card collection after he died. She had no idea it was valuable. The card was in good condition. I looked it up in a book once, and the book said it was worth ten thousand dollars.

I didn't want to give the card back. Someday, I thought, I would use that card. My dad had told me the story of the called shot many times. It fascinated me. Someday, I thought, when my mom felt I was old enough, I would travel through time again. I would see with my own eyes whether or not the Babe called his famous home run in the 1932 World Series. If I gave the card back to Dad and he sold it, I would never get the chance.

That's when I came up with an idea.

I ran down the stairs with the Ruth card in my hand. Mom and Dad were standing around awkwardly, trying to make small talk.

"Instead of giving you the card," I suggested, "what if I *use* it?"

"What do you mean, use it?" Mom asked suspiciously.

"You mean use it to go back in time?" Dad asked.

"Yeah. I could go back to 1932 and bring back a bunch of cards. You'll make a lot more money than if you just sold this one."

"Absolutely not!" my mother exclaimed. "We talked about this, Joey. I won't have you going back in time anymore."

"Aw, Mom!"

"Why not?" Dad asked.

"Because it's too dangerous, that's why not," Mom explained. "What if Joey got stuck in the 1930s? Or killed?"

"I'm not going to get killed," I insisted. "Please, Mom?"

"No!"

"I don't want to give the card back," I protested. "It will be so easy for me to just travel back to

1932, grab some old baseball cards, and bring them back with me. Dad could sell them for a lot of money."

"You see what you started?" Mom glared at Dad.

"What did *I* do?" Dad asked, holding his hands up innocently.

"You started him on this stupid card collecting."

"It's not stupid!" I chimed in.

"Well," Dad said, "what if I went back *with* Joe?"

"You mean, back to 1932?" I asked.

"Yeah. Can we do that? Can you take someone with you?"

"I don't know," I admitted. I had never tried to take anyone with me.

"You hardly spend any time with Joey in the *present,*" Mom complained. "You expect to take care of him in the *past?*"

"I'm unemployed now," Dad said. "I've got plenty of time. I'll take good care of the boy, Terry. I *am* his father."

Mom shook her head and let out a sigh.

"How long will it take?" she asked.

"A few days," I replied.

"I'll give you three days," she told Dad. "If Joey's not back in three days, I will never let you take him anywhere again."

Big deal, I thought. *He hardly ever takes me anywhere anyway.*

"We'll be back," Dad said. "I promise."

I had mixed feelings about taking Dad back in

time with me. It would be awkward hanging out with him, I knew. But it might give us a chance to get to know each other again, too. And who knew? Maybe I would be able to find out why he was so angry all the time. I walked Dad to the door and asked him when we would leave for our trip to 1932.

"Tomorrow."

3

Going Back . . .
Back . . . Back . . .

WHEN DAD CAME OVER THE NEXT DAY, I ALMOST DIDN'T recognize him. He was wearing a dark brown suit that looked a little too big on him, a vest, and a tie. He had on two-toned shoes and a hat that looked like the kind gangsters wear in old movies.

"How do I look, Butch?" he asked when I opened the door. "Pretty snazzy threads, huh?"

He handed me a big cardboard box and told me to open it. Inside was a wool sports jacket, a flat cap with a very small brim, and a pair of navy wool pants. The pants weren't long enough to be long pants, but they weren't short enough to be shorts, either.

"What's up with this?" I asked, holding up the pants.

"They're knickers," he replied. "If you want to fit in, you've got to dress the part. I did a little research to find out what boys wore in 1932."

"They dressed like dorks," I said, taking off my jeans and pulling on the knickers. I think even Mom would have gotten a laugh out of seeing me and Dad all dressed up. But she was out grocery shopping.

"Back in the 1930s, this was cool," Dad said.

Dad took out a thick wallet and opened it for me. It was stuffed with bills. My dad doesn't have a lot of money. He must have taken his life savings out of the bank.

"There's more hidden in my sock," he revealed. "And it's all old currency. I know a guy who collects the stuff."

"Why do you need to bring along so much cash?" I asked.

"I worked out a plan, Joe. I figure if we're going to do this thing, we should do it right. Make some *serious* money. First, when we get to 1932, we're going to find a bank and deposit five thousand bucks."

"What for?"

"Because if we deposit five thousand bucks, it will start earning interest in 1932. Then, when we get home and I go back to the same bank seventy years later, that five thousand will have grown. If it earns just five percent interest, in seventy years it will be worth more than *a hundred and sixty thousand dollars!* I figured it out on a computer."

"Wow! That's pretty smart, Dad."

"Oh, I'm just getting started," Dad continued excitedly. "After we deposit the money in the bank, we're going to find a bookmaker."

"Somebody who makes books?"

"No, somebody who takes bets. A bookie. I know the Yankees are going to win the 1932 World Series in four straight games. It's in the history books. I even know the final score of all the games. But they don't know this stuff in 1932 until after the games are played. I'll be able to place a bet on the Series and make a fortune."

"Dad, you're a genius!"

"Finally," he continued, "if we're lucky enough to get close to Babe Ruth at all, we're going to get him to sign as many bats, balls, and gloves as we can. That stuff is worth a pile of money in today's memorabilia market. One baseball signed by the Babe sells for about five thousand bucks."

Even as I marveled at my dad's moneymaking schemes, they made me feel a little bad. I didn't think it was illegal or anything, but it seemed slightly dishonest to go back in time and use what you know about the future to make a lot of money.

What made me feel worse was that it was all my idea to begin with. Dad saw the look on my face.

"Joe," he said, "I'm getting desperate. I've tried my hardest to make an honest living. I really did. It hasn't worked out. Think of this as a way we can help each other. You help me make a few bucks, and I help you go to 1932 to see if Babe called his shot. What's wrong with that?"

Nothing, I decided. Dad and I sat down on the

living room couch next to each other. I took the Ruth card out of its plastic holder.

"How do we do this?" Dad asked. "Do I hold the card, too?"

"The power isn't in the card," I told him. "It's in *me*. To take you along, there has to be a connection between you and me."

I hadn't held hands with my dad in years, but there was no other way. I put out my hand and he took it. His palm was sweaty. So was mine. I held the Ruth card in my other hand.

"Close your eyes," I instructed. I closed mine, too. Almost immediately, I felt the tingling.

"Do you feel anything?" I asked.

"Yeah, a weird sensation," Dad replied, "like my foot's asleep, but it's my hand."

"Wait!" I said suddenly, dropping the card.

"What's the matter?"

"I forgot something."

I ran up to my room and grabbed a new pack of baseball cards from my desk drawer.

"They have bathrooms in 1932, y'know," Dad joked when I got back.

"I didn't go to the bathroom," I explained. "A baseball card is like a plane ticket for me. The Ruth card will send us to 1932. But it won't get us back *home*. We need to bring a *new* card with us for that. If I didn't have one with me, we would have been stuck in 1932 forever."

I slipped the new pack of cards into my pocket and sat on the couch again.

"Is there anything else you forgot?" Dad asked, a little annoyed.

"No, let's do it."

I picked up the Ruth card again and grabbed Dad's hand. We closed our eyes. The tingling sensation started right up again. I visualized Babe Ruth and the 1932 World Series. *If only I could go there,* I thought.

"Feel it?" I asked Dad.

"I feel it," he replied. "It's working. . . ."

And then everything faded away.

4

Blown Off Course

WHEN I OPENED MY EYES, WE WERE NO LONGER SITTING
on the living room couch. We were sitting outdoors
on a hard bench. A big car whizzed by, spraying a
cloud of exhaust over us. It was a big, boxy old
car, with the spare tire mounted right outside the
passenger side. The tire had a bunch of spokes in
it, like a bicycle tire.

"It worked!" marveled Dad. "It really worked!"

I looked up. The building across the street
stretched up and down the block. More boxy old
cars streamed down the street. It felt chilly out,
much colder than it had been back in Louisville.

"We must be in Chicago, Joe," Dad said excitedly. "Chicago in 1932. Look at the cars! There's a
1931 Bentley Tourer. And a 1929 Pierce-Arrow."

We got up and started walking, staring at the
buildings and the cars rushing past. Louisville was

a big city, but it was nothing like *this*. I had never been to Chicago.

On the corner was a boy about my age. He was holding up a newspaper.

"Yanks beat Cubs in Game Two!" he shouted. "Read all about the World Series!"

Dad picked up a paper from the pile on the newsboy's wooden box.

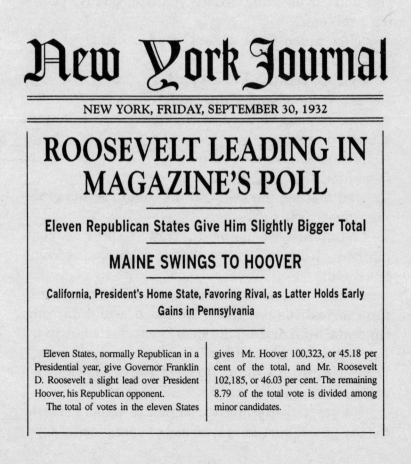

New York Journal

NEW YORK, FRIDAY, SEPTEMBER 30, 1932

ROOSEVELT LEADING IN MAGAZINE'S POLL

Eleven Republican States Give Him Slightly Bigger Total

MAINE SWINGS TO HOOVER

California, President's Home State, Favoring Rival, as Latter Holds Early Gains in Pennsylvania

Eleven States, normally Republican in a Presidential year, give Governor Franklin D. Roosevelt a slight lead over President Hoover, his Republican opponent.

The total of votes in the eleven States gives Mr. Hoover 100,323, or 45.18 per cent of the total, and Mr. Roosevelt 102,185, or 46.03 per cent. The remaining 8.79 of the total vote is divided among minor candidates.

"Hey, why are you selling the *New York Journal?*" he asked the boy.

The kid looked at Dad suspiciously. "Faw da fun of it, Mac. I'm really a millionaire. Ya wanna paper or not?"

"Are we in New York City or Chicago?" I asked the newsboy.

He gave me the same look he gave to Dad. "If you don't even know where you are, buddy, ya got big problems."

"How much for a paper?" Dad asked.

"Two cents, Mac."

Dad flipped the kid a quarter.

"Keep the change," he said.

The newsboy looked at the quarter as if it were a piece of gold.

"Thanks, mister!" Suddenly he was a lot friendlier.

Dad hustled me away, and I could see the growing anger in his eyes.

"What are we doing in New York?" he complained. "Ruth called his shot in Chicago, at Wrigley Field."

"I don't know!" I was mad, too. "It's not like in the movies! It's not like I can turn a dial on some time machine and land exactly where I want to go. I got us to 1932, didn't I?"

"All right, all right, let's both calm down," Dad said, still angry.

He started flipping through the paper, looking for the sports section, I guessed. There was no separate sports section the way newspapers have today. Finally, Dad found the few pages of the paper that were devoted to sports. Most of the sports coverage was about the World Series.

This is what the lead article said . . .

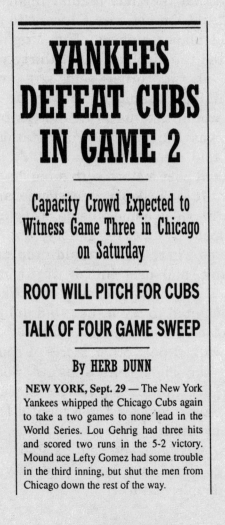

YANKEES DEFEAT CUBS IN GAME 2

Capacity Crowd Expected to Witness Game Three in Chicago on Saturday

ROOT WILL PITCH FOR CUBS

TALK OF FOUR GAME SWEEP

By HERB DUNN

NEW YORK, Sept. 29 — The New York Yankees whipped the Chicago Cubs again to take a two games to none lead in the World Series. Lou Gehrig had three hits and scored two runs in the 5-2 victory. Mound ace Lefty Gomez had some trouble in the third inning, but shut the men from Chicago down the rest of the way.

"You must have messed up somehow," Dad said, barely disguising his disgust. "We have to find a way to get to Chicago for Game Three on Saturday."

"Maybe we can fly," I suggested quietly.

"I doubt that they had regular flights in 1932," Dad said. "And I'm not sure I'd want to get on one of those old planes anyway. The Wright brothers only invented the airplane about thirty years ago."

A sign at the corner said 12TH STREET. We started walking, looking for a taxi or a subway train that would take us to Grand Central Terminal. That was the famous train station in New York, Dad told me.

We walked past a store with a big PENNY ARCADE sign on it. It was like a video game arcade, but there were no video games inside. They had simple pinball games, a shooting gallery, and these big wooden boxes where people could drop in a penny, turn a crank, and peer into a tiny window. Dad said they were called nickelodeons, like the TV channel. I wanted to try it, but Dad didn't seem to be in the mood for stopping.

As we walked past other stores, I couldn't help but notice the signs—MEN'S SHOES: $8.50. MEN'S SUITS: $25. BREAKFAST: 25 CENTS. Somebody was renting an apartment for $50 a month. Dad's mood seemed to brighten.

"Look at *this,* Joe," he said excitedly. "In 1932, you could go to the movies for just fifty cents . . . and see a double feature!"

We walked silently. I had an idea what might be going through his head. Back home, he had no job, no wife, no life, and big bills. With his life savings, he could live like a king in 1932.

I didn't say anything. If he wanted to stay in 1932, it was fine with me. I hardly ever saw him anyway.

It would have been easy for the two of us to part company right there. I could have used my new baseball cards to go back home, and Dad could have started his life over again in 1932.

But suddenly we heard a commotion down the street, around the corner. People were yelling and chanting. Something was going on.

5

Hooverville

DAD AND I TURNED THE CORNER OFF FIFTH AVENUE, AND there, in the middle of New York City, was a park. It surprised me, and I think it surprised Dad too. A small sign read UNION SQUARE PARK.

But there was no playground or anything. Nobody was playing ball or lounging in the sun in this park.

One side of the park had a row of rickety shacks made out of packing cases and sheets of scrap metal. One of them was painted with the words WELCOME TO HOOVERVILLE. Inside one of the shacks, a lady and two kids were warming their hands over a fire they had made in a metal garbage can.

As soon as we entered the park, a couple of guys with scraggly hair and worn clothing surrounded us. They held out their hands and asked politely, "Got any spare change?" Dad gave each of them a nickel, which made them extremely happy.

"We sure ain't gonna find Babe Ruth here," Dad said, annoyed.

As we walked into the park, I saw people selling pencils and old ladies selling fruit from baskets. Guys were sleeping on the grass, wrapped in overcoats.

As we walked into the park, I saw people selling pencils and old ladies selling fruit from baskets.

Some people were just wandering around with nothing to do. They had dazed, hopeless looks on their faces, like they had survived an earthquake and didn't know what to do next.

"I completely forgot," Dad said, staring at some men who were washing their clothes in a fountain. "The Depression—1932 was the worst of it."

I had heard about the Depression, but didn't know much about it. Dad told me that in 1929 the stock market crashed, sending America—and the whole world—into a Depression. Rich people became penniless overnight. Thousands of companies went out of business, and millions of people lost their jobs.

People had no money. Farmers stopped growing crops because nobody could afford to buy them. Factories shut down because people weren't buying any goods. Hundreds of people waited in lines to apply for a single job or get a loaf of bread. There was no welfare back then, no help for people who were in need.

Kids starved. A lot of people just gave up and killed themselves. It went on like that for years.

Half of me wanted to get out of the park, but the other half was fascinated by it all. We walked around. At the corner of the park on the sidewalk a row of six or seven people stood on wooden crates, each crate about twenty feet apart. They were making speeches, and small groups of people gathered around them to listen. From a distance, the voices of the speakers blended into one another, but as we got closer, I could see that each one had his own message.

"I fought in the Great War!" a man shouted. "Now I can't buy corn to feed my family."

"My brother's a farmer in Iowa," a guy yelled back. "He can't make a living selling corn for just eight cents a bushel!" Some people booed, and somebody threw a rock at the guy whose brother was a farmer.

"Tell your brother to plow his corn under!" somebody hollered. "Tell him to show the government he won't stand for it."

"If the government won't give us food, I say we just take it," an angry man yelled. "We've waited long enough."

"We've got to unionize," another speaker shouted. "That's the answer."

"God is the answer," a lady commented.

"Roosevelt is the answer," an old man hollered.

"No, Communism is the answer," said somebody else.

"Let's march on City Hall!"

"It's all President Hoover's fault. The sooner we get him out of the White House, the sooner the recovery will begin! A vote for Roosevelt is a vote for America."

"A vote for Roosevelt is a vote for the rich!" said somebody else.

Two policemen came along and tried to calm people down. They had the opposite effect. Somebody threw a rock at one of them, and it bounced off his helmet. The cop pulled out a nightstick and hit a guy with it.

"Leave me alone!" the guy yelled, holding the side of his head. "I'm just exercisin' my freedom of speech."

"Your freedom of speech ends at my ears," the cop replied.

"That ain't right," a lady said.

The people in the crowd began to hiss and boo and throw things at the cops. The second cop pulled out his pistol and fired it up in the air. The boom echoed off the buildings at the sides of the park. That shut everybody up, at least for a moment.

"Dad," I whispered, "I'm afraid."

"We'd better get out of here before we get killed," Dad said, pushing his way through the crowd. I was right behind him, tightly holding on to the back of his coat so we wouldn't be separated.

I was feeling scared and guilty. I never meant for us to see all this. All I wanted was to see Babe Ruth hitting his called-shot home run. What had gone wrong?

We were making our way through the crowd when a roar went up at the other end of the park. I tried to see what it was, but I wasn't tall enough to look over the heads of all the people around me.

"What is it, Dad?"

"I can't tell," Dad replied. "A big car just drove up."

A teenage boy had climbed a tree near us and he was squinting his eyes, peering toward the commotion.

"Hey, look!" the boy shouted. "It's Babe Ruth!"

6

The Babe

FIRST I SAW THE CAR. IT WAS A HUGE MAROON THING, AND it was honking like a flock of geese.

"It's a Packard Roadster," Dad yelled to me over the cheering of the crowd. "Twelve cylinders. Custom built. Whitewalls. Beautiful machine."

We pressed to get closer. The crowd surged around the car like iron filings around a magnet.

"It's him," Dad said, beaming like a little boy. "Feast your eyes, Butch. You're seein' the great Babe Ruth in person."

I'm not very good with faces. Sometimes I have to see somebody's face six or seven times before I recognize him. Once I was in the supermarket with my mom when my second grade teacher walked by. I had no idea who she was.

But the instant I saw Babe Ruth's face, I knew

exactly who *he* was. I'd seen his face in so many pictures.

I'm not very good with faces. But the instant I saw Babe Ruth's face, I knew exactly who *he* was.

His head was impossibly large and round. It was just about as wide as it was long. Ink-black hair fell casually across his forehead. His eyes seemed tiny compared to the rest of his head, but they were bright and laughing. His thick lips, wrapped around a big cigar, curved up in a wide grin. His nose was flattened, each nostril easily the size of a quarter. He was not a good-looking man. But the people gathered around as if he were a movie star.

"Hey, everybody!" the Babe hollered in a deep, booming voice. "Didja hear about the ball game?"

He had a slight Southern accent. He said the words "ball game" like "bowl game." A cheer went up from the crowd when he spoke.

"Did we whup them Cubbies today, or what?" bellowed the Babe. The crowd cheered louder.

"Two down and two to go, Babe!" some guy hollered.

There was a guy in the passenger seat of the car, but I didn't know who he was. Babe stood up on his seat and waved. He was wearing a brown cloth coat. Even so, I could tell he was a tall, heavy man with a beer belly. He resembled a big bear.

"We'll beat them bums in Chicago on Saturday and Sunday," Babe promised, "and bring that world championship back to New York where it belongs!"

The crowd erupted in cheers again. I looked around. Fathers were hoisting their little kids up on their shoulders to get a look at the Babe. Women were swooning. Some people just stared at him, mesmerized. It was like the biggest rock star in the world happened to stop by.

The bad feelings that had gripped the crowd earlier were gone. It didn't seem like a riot anymore. It seemed like a parade. Everybody was happy suddenly. Somebody tossed Babe a straw hat and he put it on.

"You oughta run for president, Bambino!" some guy shouted. "Hoover and Roosevelt are bums!"

The bad feelings that had gripped the crowd earlier were gone. It was like the biggest rock star in the world happened to stop by.

"That's not a bad idea." Babe chortled, his big belly shaking.

"Vote for Ruth!" people began to chant. "Vote for Ruth!"

People had started pulling pencils and scraps of

paper from their pockets. Kids pressed forward to hand them to the Babe. Patiently, he signed one for a little girl, carefully writing his name and saying a few words to her. As he accepted the next scrap of paper, the girl looked at the autograph like it was a million-dollar bill.

"Ask him for an autograph, Joe," Dad said.

I was a little embarrassed. "*You* ask him," I said.

"He's supposed to be a sucker for kids," Dad pointed out. "*You* ask him."

Babe was still signing away for the people pressed against his car. I patted my pockets. All I could come up with was the pack of baseball cards I had brought with me to get us home.

"I could have him sign a card," I suggested.

"Forget that," Dad snorted. "Imagine trying to convince a card dealer that Babe Ruth signed a baseball card from the twenty-first century."

"Just a few more, kids!" Babe yelled. "I gotta go."

Dad and I looked around on the ground frantically to see if we could find a scrap of paper. But everybody had scooped them up already.

I think Dad and I saw it at the same moment. A little boy ran by. As he passed us, a piece of paper fell out of his pocket. The boy didn't notice. I pounced on the paper.

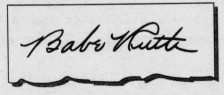

"Way to go, Joe!" Dad exclaimed, slapping me five.

Dad and I were congratulating each other when this guy came over to us. He was a tall guy, much bigger than my dad.

"I believe that belongs to my son," the guy told Dad.

"Finders keepers," I said.

It was probably not the smartest thing to say. The guy reached into his jacket and pulled out a knife. The blade was about eight inches long. I stepped back instinctively. My heart was suddenly pounding.

"How's about I cut off your @#$% hand?" the guy said, "and we'll see who finds *that?*"

"Leave my boy alone!" Dad shouted, stepping forward as he pushed me out of the way of the knife.

"Okay, I'll cut off *your* @#$% hand if you don't give back my son's autograph."

"Watch your language," Dad said. "Kids don't have to hear that kind of talk."

"Forget it, Daddy," the little boy said. "That boy can have it."

"Here," I said, handing the kid the paper. "It's not a big deal."

"Smart boy," the kid's father said as he slipped the knife back in his jacket. "Come on, Jimmy. Let's go."

It wasn't until they walked away that I realized

how fast my heart was racing. I had to take a few deep breaths to calm myself down. By that time, Babe Ruth had roared off in his Packard. Our chance to get his autograph was gone. The crowd began to break up.

"You okay, Joe?" my dad asked, putting a hand on my shoulder.

"Yeah, thanks, Dad."

"For what?"

"For sticking up for me."

"What did you think I was gonna do?" Dad asked. "Just stand there and do nothing?"

I didn't say so, but that was exactly what I'd thought he would do.

As we were walking away, another guy came over and tapped me on the shoulder. He said his name was Christy Walsh and that he was "an associate of Mr. Ruth." I recognized him as the guy who'd been sitting in the car next to Babe.

"Mr. Ruth saw what happened a few minutes ago," Walsh said. "He felt bad and asked me to tell you to stop by his suite at the Ansonia Hotel tonight. He'll give you all the autographs you want."

"We'll be there!" Dad exclaimed, pumping the guy's hand vigorously.

When Walsh disappeared into the crowd of faces on the street, Dad and I looked at each other and laughed.

"We're gonna meet Babe Ruth!" I said gleefully.

"And get all the autographs we want!" Dad said, just as happily. I don't think the two of us had shared a laugh since I was about six or seven years old.

7

Three Strikes You're Out

THE ANSONIA HOTEL, WE FOUND OUT, WAS ON SEVENTY-fourth Street. We were at Fourteenth Street. So we had to go sixty blocks to get to Babe Ruth's hotel. We started walking uptown.

Just around the corner from Union Square Park was a large building with four round columns in front of it. The sign on the front read: NEW YORK SAVINGS AND LOAN.

A line of people outside the front door of the bank stretched all the way down the street. It looked as if they were waiting for the bank to open. That was strange, Dad said, because it was already past closing time. He checked his money. If the bank was still open, he said, he'd deposit his five thousand dollars and let it earn interest for the next seventy years.

"I want my money!" a young guy yelled angrily as we got closer.

"Open the doors!" an old lady shouted.

"Give us back our money!" a group of people chanted. "Give us back our money!"

Dad pushed up to the front door and asked the young guy what was going on.

"They won't let us in," he complained. "I want to take out my money."

"Isn't it past closing time?" Dad asked.

"We want our money!" somebody yelled.

"Y'know," Dad told the guy, "if you just leave that money in the bank and wait long enough, you'll eventually be rich."

The people in the front of the line looked at Dad angrily and began shouting.

"Who asked you, pal?"

"What do you know, you idiot?"

"Mister, I don't have time to wait around," the young guy told Dad. "I need money to buy dinner *tonight*. My kids are hungry now."

"You look like *you* got plenty of dough, you with them fancy clothes," a lady shouted at Dad. "How about sharing the wealth?"

"Yeah!"

I was afraid they were going to start beating up Dad or something and take his money. But suddenly the front door of the bank opened a crack. Everybody rushed to get back in line.

"Go home!" a voice called from inside. "This bank is officially closed."

"Closed? Until when?" a lady wearing a tattered coat asked desperately.

"Until forever!" came the reply. The door slammed shut in her face.

The mob of people started pounding on the door. Four policemen mounted on horses arrived quickly, so Dad and I didn't stick around. Neither did most of the people in line. Nobody would be putting their money in or taking it out of that bank for a long time.

"That's only strike one," Dad said as we walked up Fifth Avenue. "We're not out yet."

"Don't we have to get to Chicago for Game Three, Dad?"

"Relax," my father said. "They're not going to start the game without Babe Ruth, and he's still in New York."

We passed Eighteenth Street, Twentieth Street, and Twenty-third Street, where we saw that famous building that looks like a big iron. Every so often Dad would tap a stranger on the shoulder and whisper something into the stranger's ear. Usually he would just shrug his shoulders.

"What are you doing, Dad?" I finally asked.

"Trying to find us a bookie," he replied.

After getting five or six shrugs from people, Dad tapped a guy on the shoulder who nodded his head and pointed to a nearby store. The sign on the front said: J. B. MILLER, HABERDASHER.

"Is a haberdasher the same as a bookie?" I asked as I followed Dad to the doorway.

"No," Dad replied. "Betting on baseball is illegal, so bookies set up regular businesses and take bets quietly, when the cops aren't looking."

A haberdasher, I discovered as soon as we walked in the door, is a hat salesman. I had never even seen a hat store before, but it occurred to me that every man on the street in 1932 was wearing a hat. This place had hats all over the walls. Dad leaned over to the fat guy behind the counter.

"I need to speak with Ralphie," Dad said.

"I sell hats," the guy said. "Who sent you?"

"Mike sent me."

"I'm Ralphie."

"I want to place a bet on the World Series," Dad said.

"I'm listening," Ralphie replied.

"I want to put down five thousand bucks on the Yankees to win in four straight."

Ralphie laughed. He laughed so hard he had to hold his stomach with one hand and wipe the tears rolling down his cheeks with the other.

"What's so funny?" Dad asked, annoyed. "You're a bookie, aren't you?"

"Buddy," Ralphie said, "I wish I could take your bet. But nobody's betting on the Cubs. Everybody knows the Yanks are gonna mop the floor with them in Game Three and Game Four."

"I'll give you good odds," Dad said.

"It don't matter, mister. Nobody'll take your action."

"I even know the final score of Games Three and Four."

"Forget it, pal. Take my advice. Save your money and buy yourself a hat."

We left the hat store and continued walking in the direction of Seventy-fourth Street and the Ansonia Hotel.

"Strike two," Dad said, a little dejectedly.

"You're not out yet, Dad," I said, trying to cheer him up. "Hey, why don't you bet on the presidential election? Franklin Roosevelt is going to win, isn't he?"

"That's not a bad idea, Butch," Dad replied. "But then we'd have to hang around here until Election Day to collect our money. That's next month. I promised your mom I'd have you home within three days. Besides, I have one more idea that could make us a pile of money. This one is *sure* to work."

"Dad, are you calling your shot?" I teased.

My dad struck a batting pose and pointed across the street the same way Babe Ruth supposedly pointed to the centerfield bleachers. The sign on the window said: DAVIS SPORTING GOODS—BASEBALL EQUIPMENT. GOLF CLUBS. DUMBELLS.

Dad must have realized he wasn't going to make a fortune by putting money in a bank for seventy years or by betting on the World Series. To be honest, they both sounded like crackpot ideas, once I took the time to think them through.

We walked across the street to the sporting goods store and went inside. It didn't look like any sporting goods store I'd ever seen. There were no sneakers, treadmills, or roller hockey gear. They did have these things that looked like leather beach balls. When I went to pick one up, it was so heavy I couldn't lift it. Dad said it was called a "medicine ball," and people exercised by throwing them at each other. It sounded like the dumbest thing in the world to me.

Dad marched up to the counter with a determined look on his face.

"Do you sell baseballs?" he asked.

"Certainly, sir," the clerk replied.

"Good. I want to buy a hundred of your best baseballs."

"A hundred, sir?" The clerk looked like Dad had just asked for a hundred fresh dinosaur eggs.

"That's right," Dad repeated, "a hundred."

The clerk looked flustered and said he'd have to check the stockroom.

"Looks like strike three, Dad," I said.

"It ain't over till it's over," he replied.

While the clerk scurried to the back of the store to see how many baseballs he could round up, Dad explained his strategy to me.

"A clean ball with Babe Ruth's signature on it is worth five thousand dollars in our time," he told me. "The guy in the car with Ruth said Babe would give us as many autographs as we want."

I figured it out in my head. A hundred baseballs at five thousand dollars each would earn Dad five hundred thousand dollars. *Half a million dollars!*

Not a bad payday, especially for a guy who didn't have a job.

After a few minutes the clerk returned carrying a large canvas sack, sort of like a laundry bag.

"We only have seventy-five baseballs in stock," he apologized. "They're one dollar apiece." He opened the sack to show us it was filled with cardboard boxes, each one containing a dozen baseballs.

"I'll take 'em all," Dad said, peeling bills out of his wallet. Some of the other employees in the store were staring. I did a quick mental calculation and figured out that those seventy-five balls, with Ruth's signature on them, would be worth $375,000. Dad paid the seventy-five dollars and led me out of the store.

"I think I just hit a grand slam, Butch," Dad said cheerfully as we walked uptown. "Let's head for the Ansonia and turn these baseballs into cash."

8

Payday

"ANSONIA HOTEL," DAD INSTRUCTED THE TAXICAB DRIVER. We had hailed the cab when Dad got tired of lugging around the sack filled with seventy-five baseballs.

"And step on it!" I barked. I had never been in a cab before, and I always wanted to say "step on it" to a cabdriver the way they do in the movies. It was a big, yellow car. A Studebaker, Dad told me.

The cab stopped at the corner of Broadway and Seventy-fourth Street, in front of a big old building. The corner of the building was rounded and it was really fancy. The cab fare was only a dollar. Dad handed the driver a five-dollar bill.

"Keep the change," I told the driver. I always wanted to say that, too. Dad shot me a look, but he couldn't help but chuckle. It was fun throwing a few dollars around when we knew we were about to make thousands.

The cab stopped at the corner of Broadway and Seventy-fourth Street, in front of the Ansonia Hotel.

The driver hopped out of the cab and ran around to open the door for us. *"Thankyouthankyou-thankyou,"* he kept repeating.

"We're here to see Mr. Ruth," Dad told the doorman in front of the Ansonia Hotel as he slipped a dollar into his hand.

"Seventh floor, sir. Thank you, sir!"

When the elevator door opened on the seventh floor, it was like there was a New Year's Eve party going on. The apartment door was open and people were spilling out all over the place, wandering in

and out of every room. They didn't look like baseball players. There were guys in suits and ties,
women all dressed up, bums in rags, and all kinds
of other people in between.

Nobody paid much attention to me and Dad.
They were all talking, laughing, dancing to music
that was coming out of one of those old-time record
players with a huge horn attached to it. A tele-
phone was ringing constantly, and nobody bothered
picking it up. Babe Ruth was nowhere to be seen.

Dad and I walked around. The apartment was
way bigger than my house back home. There must
have been ten or eleven rooms. It took up the entire
seventh floor of the Ansonia. None of the rooms had
TV sets, but most of them had a radio that was the
size of a TV set.

"Why are there pots all over the floor?" I yelled
to Dad over the crowd noise.

"They're spittoons," Dad shouted back. "You spit
tobacco juice into them."

Sure enough, I saw some guy lean back and
launch a stream of brown goop into a spittoon from
ten feet away. It was an amazing shot to me, but
nobody else seemed to be impressed.

We looked all over the place but couldn't find
Babe Ruth. Dad noticed a door to one of the rooms
was closed. He winked at me, knocked softly on the
door, and opened it.

The Babe wasn't in there, either. Two girls were
sitting on a couch. They looked up at us. One of
them looked a little older than me, the other one a

bit younger. They were doing their homework, it seemed. A lady, who must have been their mother, was reading in a chair.

"Oh, I'm sorry," Dad said, backing out of the door. "We're looking for Mr. Ruth."

"Daddy's in the kitchen, most likely," one of the girls said.

We closed the door, looked at each other, and mouthed the word "Daddy?" to each other. I never knew Babe Ruth *had* kids.

It took some time, but we finally pushed our way through the throng of people jamming the hallway to get to the kitchen. Sure enough, there was the Babe, in the middle of everybody. He was in his street clothes—brown pants, tan shirt.

"Watch this!" the Babe boomed. He was chomping on a cigar, and he had a baseball bat in his hand. He held it over his head, straight up and down. Then he leaned back and put the knob end of the bat on his nose. When he had the bat balanced, he took his hands off it.

"One . . . two . . . three . . . four . . ." everybody counted.

The Babe kept balancing the bat on his nose. Soon the bat wobbled a bit, and Babe moved his head to the right to keep the bat steady. He went a little too far, and the bat wobbled the other way. It was impossible for him to balance it anymore. Before the chant reached *"seven,"* the bat toppled over and clonked him right on the head.

Everybody laughed, but I didn't. I rushed over to the big man.

"Are you okay, Babe?"

Babe let out a big laugh and rubbed his head. "Solid rock!" he chortled. Most of the people had streamed away into other rooms, as if the show was over.

"Mr. Ruth," Dad said, stepping forward, "my name is Bill Stoshack and this young man is my son, Joe. Do you remember us?"

Babe stuck out his hand to shake. It was enormous. He had big calluses on his fingers, I guess from gripping bats.

"Sure, you're the kid I nearly ran over today on Riverside Drive! Gee, I'm sorry about that, kid. Gotta be more careful."

"No," I said. "That must have been somebody else."

"Are you the kid who asked me to come to his confirmation?"

"Uh, no."

"Babe," Dad interrupted, "Joe tried to get your autograph when you drove by Union Square Park today, and some man pulled a knife on him."

"Oh yeah!" Babe roared. "I remember you! You're my lucky charm, kid. That guy coulda been planning to stab me. You mighta saved my life."

I really didn't think Babe Ruth remembered me at all. But I didn't care. There I was, in his apartment, talking with him! I had actually shaken hands with the great Babe Ruth! How many kids could say that? I was so happy, I didn't care if I got to see the called shot or not.

"Babe," Dad piped up, "seeing as how Joe saved your life and all, would you mind signing some autographs for him?"

"Sure, Pop," Babe said. "Whatcha got in the bag? Toys for all the kiddies? Christmas ain't for two months."

"Not quite."

Dad opened the sack and Babe leaned over to peer inside. He whistled when he saw all the boxes of baseballs.

"You don't have to sign them *all*," I said apologetically, which made Dad shoot me one of his angry looks.

"Hey, you didn't have to save my life either," Babe replied. "C'mon."

He led us to a quiet room and shut the door behind us. Sitting down at the desk, he dumped out all the boxes of baseballs. Then he pulled a fountain pen from his pocket and signed the first ball in a smooth, flowing line. I noticed he wrote right-handed, even though he threw and batted left-handed.

As Babe picked up the next ball, I peeked at Dad. There weren't any dollar signs flashing in his eyes or anything, but there might as well have been.

One by one, Babe picked up each ball and signed it. I would have thought he would be sick of writing his name on things for people. But he didn't

One by one, Babe picked up each ball and signed it. He didn't know it, but that bag of baseballs was now worth $375,000.

complain. He didn't make up an excuse so he could leave. He didn't ask for any money, the way today's athletes do. And he didn't stop until every single baseball had his signature on it.

Dad collected all the balls and carefully put them back in the sack. Babe didn't know it, but that bag of baseballs was now worth $375,000. Dad couldn't stop thanking him.

"I promise you," Dad said, "we will never ask you to sign anything else ever again."

Babe didn't seem to mind or care. "Hey, I'm starved," he suddenly said. "You boys want to go grab some grub? Let's get out of this dump and strap on the feedbag."

"Isn't this your party?" I asked, following him out of the room.

"Yeah, so what?" he replied, unconcerned. He pushed his way past anyone who stood between him and the door.

"Who are all these people?" Dad asked as we struggled to keep up with Babe.

"How should I know?" he said, grabbing a big furry racoon coat from the closet. "Let's go."

He was like a tornado, moving one way almost randomly and then another, sweeping up everything in his path. There was no point trying to control him. Dad grabbed the sack of baseballs and we piled into the elevator behind Babe.

It would be an adventure. I was sure of that.

9

Living Big

BABE PULLED A FLOPPY HAT FROM THE POCKET OF HIS COAT and put it on his head so it nearly covered his eyes. Still, as we rushed down Broadway behind him, people stared, pointed, and called his name. Even though he was disguised, Babe was instantly recognizable.

"I know a joint where nobody'll bother us," he said, hailing a cab.

After a few minutes, the cab pulled up to a place called Delmonico's. Babe tossed the driver a twenty-dollar bill for a seventy-five-cent fare. I thought the driver was going to faint, he was so happy. He probably didn't earn that much money in a week.

Delmonico's was a really fancy restaurant, with big mirrors and chandeliers and waiters walking around in tuxedos. When the owner spotted Babe coming in the door, he rushed over and bowed like the King of England had arrived. He led us to a private room in the back that was separated from the rest of the diners.

"Will you be having the usual, Mr. Ruth?" the waiter asked.

"Yeah," Babe agreed. "I'm so hungry I could eat a cow."

"I'll have the usual too," I chimed in.

I always wanted to say, "I'll have the usual." Babe laughed like it was the funniest thing he'd ever heard.

"Bring out your best steaks for my guests," he instructed the waiter.

"I'll have a beer to go with mine," Dad said.

"Beer?" Babe stared at Dad with an astonished look on his face. "Where have you been, Pop? Ain't-cha never heard of Prohibition? Alcohol's been illegal since 1920."

"Oh, I forgot," Dad said, embarrassed.

Babe roared with laughter. "A pitcher of beer for me and my friend," he told the waiter, "and a soda pop for the boy." Then he turned to us and whispered, "I don't like rules. Never did."

In seconds, the waiter brought out our drinks. We all clinked glasses. "To the Cubs," Dad toasted. "May you demolish them in four straight."

"Here's mud in your eye," Babe said before draining his whole glass in one gulp. "You look like a ballplayer, Pop. Ever play the game?"

"Only in high school," Dad replied. "I'm a machinist, currently between jobs."

"You and everybody else." Babe sighed. "Don't worry, Pop. The Depression will be over soon. I got a hunch Hoover's gonna find a way to beat this thing."

Dad glanced over at me. He had told me that Franklin Roosevelt would beat President Hoover in the 1932 election, and it would be many years before America would come out of the Depression.

"Me, I gotta find a way to beat them Cubbies."

"When do you leave for Chicago?" Dad asked.

"Tonight," Babe replied. "Our train leaves from Grand Central at midnight."

I snuck a peek at Dad. He glanced at his watch. If we were going to witness the called shot, we had to get on that train. We both knew it.

It wasn't long before a waiter brought out an enormous platter of food. He put steaks in front of me and Dad and then placed a semicircle of plates before the Babe.

A thick steak with a border of lamb chops around it. A whole roast chicken. A mountain of mashed potatoes. Corn. Peas. Spinach. Bread. I couldn't believe any human being would be able to eat that much food.

"Dig in, boys."

My steak was delicious, but I couldn't enjoy it. I couldn't take my eyes off Babe. He ate like a starving animal that had just made a kill. He tore at the food, ripping it apart with his knife and fork and shoveling it into his mouth. At the same time he was swallowing one mouthful, he was filling his fork with the next one, barely stopping to chew.

He emptied the entire ketchup bottle onto his plate. Food and gravy dribbled down his chin. He didn't seem to care. I was fascinated.

"Can we get some seconds over here, for crying out loud?" he bellowed when his plates were empty. More food arrived in short order, and he attacked it with nearly as much enthusiasm as he did the first helping.

Just when I thought he couldn't possibly handle another bite, he asked, "Hey kid, you eatin' that?" I told him I was finished, and he scooped what was left of the steak off my plate like a hawk diving for its prey. In seconds, he had devoured it.

"Some dessert, Mr. Ruth?" asked a waiter, who was clearing off our empty plates.

"Apple pie à la mode, my good man," Babe said, "and don't scrimp on the mode!"

Dad and I each had a sliver of pie, but Babe finished most of it himself. Then he washed everything down with another pitcher of beer.

It was an awesome performance. If someone had been there watching Leonardo da Vinci paint the *Mona Lisa,* I thought, it must have been something like this. I felt like I should give him a standing ovation.

"That hit the spot!" Babe said, satisfied, as he wiped his mouth with the corner of the tablecloth.

Then he reached into his pocket and pulled out

a bottle. The label said BICARBONATE OF SODA. Babe didn't put the white powder into a glass of water, as I expected. Instead, he just dug out a heaping spoonful of the stuff and shoved it in his mouth dry. He let it settle in his stomach for a few seconds, then let out a belch that—I swear—rattled the stained-glass window behind me. He followed that with the loudest fart I'd ever heard.

"Hey, who cut the cheese?" Babe chuckled, and then roared at his own joke.

"Y'know, Babe," Dad said, "you might think about losing a few pounds. Dieting a little. That extra weight is going to slow you down as you get older."

"Dieting?" Babe laughed. "Dieting is for guys who hit singles. You gotta *eat* big if you wanna *hit* big. And, boys, I swing big with everything I've got. I hit big or I miss big. I like to live as big as I can."

A waiter came in. He put the check on the table and left. All the food we had eaten only came to twenty-five dollars. Babe peeled off a hundred-dollar bill from his wallet and dropped it on the table like it was a quarter.

The waiter didn't rush to come and get the money, and Babe didn't seem like he was in any hurry to leave. I figured it would be a good time to pick his brain—find out if he was planning to call his shot.

"So," I said casually, "do you have any plans for Game Three? Like, specific plans?"

"Yeah, I got a plan," Babe said. I leaned forward

in my seat. Maybe he was going to tell me he would call his shot.

"My plan is to murder them Cubbies."

"I mean, do you plan to hit one out of the park, Babe?"

"Kid," Babe said, "I *always* plan to hit one out of the park."

"I mean, on one particular pitch?"

"On *every* pitch," Babe replied.

Well, I had found out one thing, anyway. The called shot was not something Babe Ruth cooked up in advance. If he was going to do it, it would be a spontaneous thing.

"Is it hot in here?" Babe asked.

As we talked, I had noticed that droplets of sweat were appearing on Babe's forehead. He pulled a handkerchief from his pocket and mopped his face with it. He seemed to be breathing heavily, and suddenly he looked very tired. His face was getting more pale every second.

"Boys," Babe said suddenly, holding the edge of the table, "I think I'm gonna be sick."

Then his eyes rolled up toward the ceiling. He toppled off his chair and hit the floor like an elephant that had been shot.

10

Playing with History

BABE RUTH HIT BIG, AND HE MISSED BIG, AND HE LIVED
big. And I can tell you this from personal experi-
ence—Babe Ruth also *puked* big.

When the Babe's body hit the restaurant floor
with a thud, Dad and I looked at each other,
speechless. We had expected to have an interesting
adventure when we traveled back to 1932. But neither of us were counting on an adventure that in-
volved Babe Ruth lying unconscious underneath
our table.

"Is he dead?"

"I don't think so."

"What should we do, Dad?" I asked, more than
slightly worried. The waiters, for a change, were
nowhere to be seen.

"Turn him on his side," Dad instructed. "We
don't want him to choke on his own vomit."

I got down on the floor and started shoving against Babe's shoulder. It was like trying to push a truck out of a snowdrift. When Dad saw me struggling, he joined me on the floor. Finally we were able to roll the big man over. He didn't wake up, but I could hear his labored breathing. At least he was alive.

"We have to clean him up and get him over to Grand Central," I told Dad, "or he won't make that midnight train to Chicago for Game Three."

I picked up Babe's limp hand to check his watch. It was just after eleven o'clock.

"Wait a minute," Dad said, thinking things over. "Game Three is in the history books, right? We *know* he got to Chicago. We *know* he hit that famous homer. Even if we do nothing, we know he's gonna get to the game somehow. Maybe we shouldn't play with history and risk messing things up. Maybe we should just leave him be."

"But, Dad, we *already* played with history. Maybe we messed history up by having dinner with him and letting him eat so much. Besides, *look* at him!"

The Babe was curled up in a ball on the floor, looking as dead as roadkill. He was making grunting noises. He was in no shape to sit up, much less hit a ninety-mile-per-hour fastball.

"You're right," Dad agreed. "This could all be our fault. If we don't help him, he might never even hit the called shot. Okay, here's what we're gonna do. You stay here and keep an eye on him. I'll go over to his apartment and get him some clean clothes. When I get back, we'll dress him and get him to Grand Central."

"Okay!" I agreed.

Dad and I looked at each other for a moment. There was a little twinkle in his eye. I'm not sure, but I kind of had the feeling that he was thinking exactly what I was thinking—this is *cool!*

Sure, Babe Ruth had passed out right in front of us and we might have messed up one of the most famous moments in sports history. But Dad and I were together, and for the first time in a long time I was actually enjoying being with him.

"You know, I was thinking," Dad said, "when this thing is all over and we get home . . ."

"Yeah?"

"Maybe we could bottle Babe's barf. Sell it for a fortune."

"You're joking, right, Dad?"

"Yeah," he said, hesitating for a moment. "I think so."

While Dad rushed back to the Ansonia to get Babe's clothes, I cleaned Babe up with ice water and cloth napkins. The water must have revived him, because after a few minutes he opened his eyes.

"What inning is it?" he asked, bewildered.

"We're still at the restaurant, Babe," I informed him. "You passed out."

"I'm a mess," he grunted, pulling himself up to

a sitting position next to his chair. "Where's your dad?"

"He went to get your clothes and suitcase."

"He's a fine man, your dad."

"I guess," I replied. I couldn't help thinking of all the times my dad hadn't been such a fine man.

"You *guess?*" Ruth snorted. "You're lucky you *got* a dad. Where are you from, kid?"

"Louisville, Kentucky."

"And your dad brought you all the way to New York? Kid, when I was a boy, my dad only took me to one place—the home."

"What home?" I asked.

"You don't want to hear my sob story."

"I do," I insisted. "What home?"

"St. Mary's. A reform school in Baltimore, where I grew up. I was only seven. Dad took me on the trolley with him one day. He dropped me off at St. Mary's and left. It was the only home I ever had. He never visited me. Not once. Not even on my birthday."

Babe was still sitting on the floor next to the table. The color had returned to his face and he looked like he was going to be all right. He was speaking softly now, more seriously. It was so different from the booming voice he used in a crowd of people. Babe seemed to relax when there weren't any grown-ups around. It almost felt like I was talking with another kid.

"Why did your dad put you in reform school?" I asked.

"I was a bad kid," he replied. "I was always getting into fights, running from the cops, refusing to go to school. My dad owned a saloon near the Baltimore docks, and I was drinking beer before I could read. One day I stole a dollar from his cash register. I used it to buy ice cream for every kid on the block. Dad caught me and beat me with a pool cue. It was probably the only attention he ever gave me. I get plenty of attention now."

"My dad would never do anything like that."

"Like I said, your dad is a good man. Nobody's perfect, but he's got a lot of good in him. I figure we should find the good in a person and try to get past the bad. Learn from the good. You don't have to copy everything about a person. Just the good things."

"How long were you in reform school?"

"Until I was nineteen. I never had a childhood. Guess that's why I act like a kid sometimes."

Babe reached into his coat pocket and pulled out a black pipe. "At least some good came out of living at St. Mary's," he said as he stuffed the pipe with tobacco. "I learned how to play ball there."

It occurred to me that Babe always had something in his mouth. A pipe, cigar, gum, chewing tobacco, something.

"Babe, you shouldn't smoke," I warned him. "It kills people."

"Kid," he said as he lit the pipe, "I had seven brothers and sisters. Six of them died when they were babies. My mother died when she was thirty-four. Tuberculosis. My father got kicked in the head in a fight outside his saloon and died when he was forty-six."

"I'm sorry," I said.

"I could get hit in the head by a fastball tomorrow," Babe said quietly. "I've seen it. I saw a man die once."

"You did?"

"We were playing Cleveland in 1920. Their little shortstop, Ray Chapman, didn't see a pitch coming at him. It busted his skull. He crumpled like a rag doll right in the batter's box. I saw it with my own eyes. A few hours later, Chapman was dead. So if you don't mind, kid, I'm gonna have a smoke."

By that time, the waiter finally arrived and helped Babe into his seat. He seemed like his old self, maybe a little more subdued. Dad came rushing in, lugging an enormous suitcase that was plastered with stickers—BALTIMORE, DETROIT, WASHINGTON, CHICAGO—just about every big city in the country.

"You're a good man, Pop," Babe said when he saw Dad.

By now I had noticed that Babe never called anyone by his name. He always called me "Kid." Dad was "Pop." Young women were "Sister" and older ones "Mom." Old men were "Doc." I guess he met so many people, he gave up trying to learn anyone's name.

"Maybe we should get you to a doctor," Dad said.

"@#$% that," Babe replied. "Pardon my French. Just get me to Grand Central."

Dad opened Babe's suitcase on the table. Babe stood up gingerly and we helped him out of his messed-up clothes. Instead of saving them to be cleaned, he just threw them into a garbage can.

Standing there in his underwear, Babe Ruth looked nothing like a ballplayer. His gut was bigger and flabbier than I'd imagined. His legs were skinny, like a bird's. He had friction burns on his thighs and hips, probably from sliding into bases. There was a big pink scar that went across his stomach. He saw me staring at it.

"I had an operation back in '25," he said. "Almost died."

"The bellyache heard 'round the world," I said, recalling my baseball books back home.

Dad and I helped Babe get dressed. He picked out a white silk shirt, brown pants, and a pair of two-toned shoes from what Dad had packed. When he pulled on the pants, he grimaced with pain.

"I'm getting too old for this, boys," he moaned.

"How old are you, Babe?" I asked.

"Thirty-seven," he replied, struggling with the zipper. "I can't run the bases anymore. Can't cover the outfield. Got a trick knee. The legs are always the first to go. That's why I only hit forty-one homers this year."

"Ever think of calling it quits, Babe?" Dad asked. "Retiring?"

"I can't." He grunted. "These are tough times

for everybody. America needs heroes. And I'm the hero."

"If you took better care of yourself," I told Babe, "I bet you'd hit a lot more homers."

"Kid, I hit sixty in one season," Babe said. "I hit almost seven hundred in my career. Nobody'll ever top that."

Dad and I glanced at each other. Neither of us wanted to tell Babe that both of those records would be topped eventually.

After he was dressed and cleaned up, Babe looked pretty good—especially for a guy who had been lying under a table unconscious a half hour earlier. Dad grabbed his sack of baseballs and I helped Babe out to the street, where he quickly hailed a cab. The cabbie took Babe's big suitcase and put it in the trunk.

"Boys," Babe said as he opened the door, "I don't know what I would have done without you." He pulled out his wallet, peeled off a hundred-dollar bill, and handed it to my dad. "I want you to have this. It's the least I can do after all you've done for me."

"We don't want any money, Babe."

I couldn't believe my ears. My dad, who seemed to spend every waking hour thinking of ways to make money, had just turned down a hundred-dollar bill. I figured I must have been hallucinating.

"How can I repay you?" Babe asked.

"Well, there is *one* way," Dad said, almost shyly. "Can you get us two tickets to Game Three?"

"Is that all?" Babe laughed, reaching into his pocket and pulling out a pair of tickets. "Sure!"

"Uh, one more thing, Babe," Dad said as Babe stepped in the cab.

"What is it, Pop?"

"Can you get us to Chicago?"

"Boys, it will be my pleasure!" Babe said. "Hop in!"

11

Dumb Luck

BY THE TIME OUR CAB GOT TO GRAND CENTRAL, IT WAS A few minutes before midnight. It looked like we were going to miss the train to Chicago. If Babe never made it to Game Three, the history of baseball would be changed forever. The called shot would never happen. And it would be my fault.

But as soon as Babe entered the station, it was like the rest of the world stopped.

"Mister Ruth! Mister Ruth!" an African-American porter called, "the Yankees are waiting for you!"

"They'd *better* wait!" Babe boomed. "Without me, they don't stand a chance against the Cubs!"

The quiet, serious Babe who had confided in me about his miserable childhood on the docks of Baltimore was suddenly gone. Like a light switch flipped on, in public he was the jovial, obnoxious Babe. He was in great spirits again, showing no signs of being sick.

The porter grabbed Babe's suitcase, and we followed him through the station. It occurred to me for the first time that all the black people I'd seen in 1932 were porters or cleaning ladies or people who did some menial job. And I knew there were no black players in the major leagues.

As we rushed through the train station, people swarmed around Babe as usual, calling his name and asking for autographs. This time he reluctantly turned down these requests, explaining that he had to catch a train so he could beat "them bums in Chicago."

The porter led us through the station to a huge train that was belching smoke and soot. On the side of the train it said TWENTIETH CENTURY LIMITED. A bunch of women spotted Babe and grabbed him to pose for a photo with them.

"Ruth!" shouted an angry-looking man standing in front of the train. "Where were you? Out carousing?"

"Who's that guy?" I asked my dad.

"Must be Joe McCarthy," he whispered back, "the Yankee manager."

"Don't get hot under the collar, Skip," Babe said casually as he stepped past McCarthy onto the train, "I'm here, ain't I?"

"All aboard!" a conductor shouted, holding a megaphone to his mouth. "All aboard for Chicago!"

"Ruth!" McCarthy demanded, putting his arm in front of us as we tried to follow Babe up the steps. "Who's this guy? Who's the kid?"

The porter led us through the station to a huge train that was belching smoke and soot. A bunch of women grabbed Babe to pose for a photo with them.

"Don't get in a tizzy, Skip. These boys are friends of mine."

"They ain't gettin' on this train!" McCarthy said angrily.

"Well," Babe said, stepping back down to the platform, "if they ain't gettin' on this train, I ain't gettin' on this train either!"

He didn't say it in exactly those words. Babe and McCarthy added about one curse word for every regular word they used. McCarthy looked at Babe with disgust. "Oh, get on the train, you fat slob!" he finally said. "I've had it up to here with you."

Babe laughed. Dad and I piled in behind him. With the Babe finally on board, the train immediately lurched forward. It would take all night and most of Friday to travel eight hundred miles from New York to Chicago. If we had been on a jet, I knew, the trip would have taken less than two hours. But in 1932, there were no jets to take.

The last three cars of the train, Babe told us, were reserved for the Yankees. One car was the dining car. A second car had rows of seats like a regular train. The third car was the sleeper. That's where Babe led us.

The sleeper car was basically a bunch of tiny enclosed rooms, just big enough for one person to sleep in. They were stacked on top of one another, like bunk beds. Veteran players like Babe got the lower berths while the younger players had to climb up to the top ones.

Those beds looked inviting. It was past midnight and I hadn't slept in I don't know how long. But who could sleep? I was too revved up. I was on my way to Chicago! With the great Babe Ruth! And the New York Yankees! To see Game Three of the 1932 World Series!

"Lemme introduce you boys to the fellas," Babe said, tossing his suitcase into his little berth.

He led us to the dining car, which was like a tiny restaurant on wheels. There was a little counter where a guy was making sandwiches. All the tables were bolted to the floor so they wouldn't slide around.

Guys were sprawled all over the place, some of them in jackets and ties and others sitting there in their underwear. Some were eating a late dinner. Some were playing cards or reading newspapers.

It was stuffy. There was no air-conditioning. Most of the guys were smoking, and the smoke hung in the air like fog. The train was chugging along now, its wheels clacking on the rails.

"Hey, Flop Ears, how's tricks?" Babe said to a guy who, I had to admit, *did* have kind of floppy ears. "Chicken Neck, you son of a gun!" he said to another guy, "what's buzzin', cousin?" To a third he asked, "We gonna beat them Cubbies, Horse Nose?"

Babe greeted all the Yankees with his personal nicknames for them. I didn't catch all of them, but I did remember "Wop," "Rubber Belly," "Duck Eye," and "Barney Google." They all greeted Babe—and me—good-naturedly. They called Babe "Jidge," I guess because his real name was George.

Dad was in awe, just staring. He's been a Yankee fan since he was a kid. I'd never seen him so excited. He was able to recognize most of the players, even though they were out of uniform.

"See that skinny guy?" he whispered to me. "That's Frank Crosetti. Third baseman. And that tall guy? That's Bill Dickey, the Hall of Fame catcher. He's from Louisiana. And there's Tony Lazzeri. Second base. He had epilepsy. And there's Earle Combs . . . Joe Sewell . . . Lefty Gomez . . ."

"Which one is Lou Gehrig?" I asked. I had heard a lot about Gehrig, because he played more than two thousand games in a row and owned the record for consecutive games until Cal Ripken Jr. broke it in the 1990s. Gehrig would have played even longer, but he got this terrible disease called amyotrophic lateral sclerosis. It's a disease that affects the spinal nerves and muscles. It forced him to retire right away. After he died, ALS came to be called Lou Gehrig's disease.

"I don't see Gehrig," Dad replied, looking around.

The players didn't pay much attention to Dad and me. I figured they were surrounded by fans all the time and considered their time on the train as their one chance to be together as a team. Babe sat at a table with a bunch of guys who were telling jokes and laughing. Dad and I sat down at another table and Dad ordered two pieces of pie.

We had been moving for only a few minutes when a kid came through the dining car. He was carrying a big tray filled with gum, chocolate, jelly beans—just about every kind of candy I could think of. He was selling them for pennies and nickels. But Babe peeled another one of those hundred-dollar bills out of his wallet and bought the kid's whole tray. Then he started tossing the candies to everyone in the car.

Somebody produced a ukulele and handed it to

Babe. He got up on his chair, sat on the counter, and began to strum. He actually knew how to play the thing. Soon he was singing "Oh! Susannah" in a deep voice that was surprisingly good. Some of the other Yankees joined in when Babe played "Jeannie With the Light Brown Hair" and "The Sidewalks of New York."

At around one o'clock some of the players got up to leave. "Come on, you party poopers!" Babe called to them. "Are you tired already?"

"Yeah," Lazzeri said, "tired of listening to your rotten singing, Jidge! You can't carry a tune in a bucket. I'm going to hit the hay."

It occurred to me how tired *I* was. My head felt heavy, like I could fall asleep in a second if I tried. Dad and I didn't have a sleeper, and there was no way we were going to fit into Babe's.

"Aren't you tired, Babe?" I asked when he came around to see how we were doing. "Maybe you should get a good night's sleep so you'll be rested for Game Three."

"Heck, no," Babe replied. "I can sleep for five months after we win the Series." He joined a card game with some of the Yankees who liked to stay up late.

Dad and I got up and went into the next car, where there were seats we could sleep on. There was just one guy in there, sitting a few rows in front of us. He was writing something on a pad of paper. I curled up against Dad the best I could. It was uncomfortable, but at least it was quieter than the dining car.

Just before I fell asleep, the guy who was sitting in front of us got up and came over. He was holding a coat.

"Excuse me," he said nervously. "I don't mean to be nosy, but I thought your boy might be able to use this as a cover."

"Thanks!" Dad said.

"Nice guy," I muttered to Dad after the guy walked away.

"Do you know who that man was, Butch?"

"No, who?" I asked.

"Lou Gehrig."

I bolted upright. Gehrig was about to leave the car, probably to go to sleep.

"Mr. Gehrig! Mr. Gehrig!" I called, getting up quickly. He stopped and turned around. It *was* Lou Gehrig! I recognized his face from photos. He looked younger than Babe, with thick, wavy hair and dimples on his cheeks when he smiled. He was wearing a white, button-down shirt.

"Can I have your autograph, Mr. Gehrig?"

"Sure, son."

I had Dad bring over one of the balls from his sack. Lou Gehrig signed it on the opposite side from where Babe had already signed it.

"Thanks!" Dad and I gushed when he handed me back the ball.

"Don't mention it."

I didn't know what to say, but I wanted to keep

He looked younger than Babe, with thick, wavy hair and dimples on his cheeks when he smiled. It was Lou Gehrig!

talking with Lou Gehrig. "What were you writing in your pad?" I asked.

"Joe!" Dad said sternly, "that's personal!"

"It's okay," Gehrig said, holding out his pad, a little embarrassed. "A letter to my mom," he admitted bashfully.

"Why weren't you in the dining car with the other players?" I asked him.

"I don't go in much for carousing with the boys and spending a lot of money," he said quietly. "I want to save it for when I'm old and gray."

I stole a look at Dad. We both knew that Lou Gehrig would never be old and gray. I didn't know what else to say. Neither did Gehrig. He seemed almost painfully shy. There was an awkward silence.

"Well, good luck in Game Three tomorrow, Mr. Gehrig," Dad said.

"I'll do my best," he said, then he disappeared into the sleeper car.

Dad admired the signed baseball. I knew that a ball signed by both Babe and Lou was worth a fortune, maybe hundreds of thousands of dollars.

"When did he get sick, Dad?" I asked.

"Nineteen thirty-nine," my father replied somberly. "Just seven years from now. Nine years from now, he's going to die. He has no idea. Nobody does."

"Maybe we can do something?"

"There's nothing we can do to help him," Dad

explained. "Seventy years from now they *still* won't have a cure for Lou Gehrig's disease."

"Of all the guys for that to happen to," I said, shaking my head. "Why did it have to be such a nice guy like Lou Gehrig?"

"You can try as hard as you want," Dad said. "Be as good as you can be. But a lot of what happens in the world is plain dumb luck."

"Scranton, Pennsylvania!" the conductor announced as the train slowed to a stop.

I leaned my head against Lou Gehrig's coat, thinking to myself that I would never complain about any silly little problems I had again. Almost immediately, I fell asleep.

12

A Secret Revealed

"NEXT STOP, LA SALLE STREET STATION, CHICAGO, Illinois!"

When I woke up, Dad was staring out the window, a sort of dreamy look on his face.

"What time is it?" I mumbled.

"About five o'clock. You slept almost the whole day."

"I guess I'm jet-legged from traveling seventy years through time."

"Do you see anything unusual out there, Butch?"

"No," I said, looking out the window. "Just a bunch of farms."

"That's right," he agreed. "A bunch of farms. No McDonald's or Burger Kings. No shopping malls. No housing developments. I was just thinking that someday this beautiful country will be paved over."

It didn't mean that much to me. I had never known anything other than a world of McDonald's and Burger Kings and malls and housing developments. Looking out the window, I had to admit the world was prettier back then.

"Do you think he'll do it?" I asked my dad.

"Do what, Butch?"

"Call his shot."

"I don't know," he said. "But we'll be there to see it if he does, won't we?"

"Tell me again when he's going to hit it, Dad."

"It will be in the fifth inning," he told me. "The score will be four-four. There will be one out. Nobody on base. The count will be two balls and two strikes. That's the pitch when Babe will hit the most famous homer in baseball history."

The hair on my arms, I realized, was standing up. I had goose pimples.

Suddenly Dad looked at me, with excitement in his eyes.

"Butch!" he exclaimed, "I just had a brainstorm!"

"What is it?"

"We'll be the only ones in Wrigley Field who will know Babe is going to hit the homer, right? We know exactly *when* he's going to hit it, and I know pretty much *where* he's going to hit it—deep to straightaway centerfield."

"So?"

"Butch, I'm going to catch that ball!"

"Catch it?"

"Yeah! I'll position you down low in the stands so you can see if Babe calls the shot or not. Then, in the fifth inning, I'll go to deep centerfield and grab the ball when it lands! I don't know why I didn't think of it sooner!"

"You're a genius, Dad!"

"Butch, do you have any idea how much the ball Babe Ruth hit for his called-shot homer will be worth someday?"

"Thousands?"

"More," Dad continued. "Remember when Mark McGwire hit seventy home runs in one season? Do you remember how much money the guy who caught number seventy sold it for?"

"A million dollars or something like that?"

"*Three* million bucks!" Dad exclaimed.

"You've *got* to catch that ball, Dad!" I said.

"I'm gonna catch that ball."

We settled into our seats and thought about what we would do if we had three million dollars. A newsboy came around selling papers, and Dad bought one. He was skimming the pages when he suddenly stopped at a page. His hands started shaking, which made the paper rustle. His breathing was heavy. I was afraid all the excitement about catching the called-shot ball had caused him to have a heart attack or something.

"What is it, Dad?" I asked.

"Nothing."

I looked to see what he was reading in the paper.

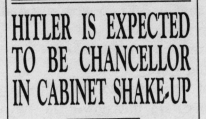

HITLER IS EXPECTED TO BE CHANCELLOR IN CABINET SHAKE-UP

Every Likelihood Now That Nazi Leader Will Be Appointed Within a Few Days

Government Seeks Assurance of Moderation and Check on Fascist Leader.

Von Papen Likely to Be Foreign Minister—Two More Killings as New Decrees Take Effect.

By CHRISTOPHER RICHMOND
Special Cable to THE JOURNAL

BERLIN — There is every likelihood tonight that within a few days Adolf Hitler will be the Chancellor of the German Republic. Thus the impossible of yesterday, in view of the attitude of the present government has become the best bet of today.

The world's greatest political poker

I knew a little bit about Adolf Hitler. I knew he was the dictator of Nazi Germany during World War II. He tried to take over the world, and he killed millions of innocent people in concentration camps. It was called the Holocaust. But I didn't know what that had to do with my dad or why he was reacting so strongly.

"What's the matter?" I asked.

"You're too young."

"I am not," I protested. "I'm thirteen."

Dad sighed. He put down the newspaper and looked at me.

"Have you ever wondered," he asked me, "why you don't have a lot of cousins or uncles or aunts on my side of the family?"

"I guess your parents and grandparents didn't have many kids."

"My grandparents had eleven children, Joe," Dad explained, "six boys and five girls."

"What happened to them?"

"They were killed," Dad said quietly. "Ten of them."

"By the Nazis?"

"My grandparents lived in Lodz, in central Poland near Warsaw," Dad explained. "A quiet little city. It must have been one crazy house, with all thirteen of them living together. The Nazis invaded Poland in September of 1939. Little by little they started rounding people up. In 1944, they took my grandparents away. The children, too. Only my father escaped, by hiding under the house. The Nazis sent the rest of the family to Treblinka, a concentration camp. They were all killed. In the gas chambers. My dad somehow made it to America. I don't know how exactly. It was never something he would talk much about."

My father exhaled deeply, like he had been holding that story in for a long time. The thought crossed my mind that maybe that was why my dad was so angry all the time. He had never gotten over what happened to his family.

He was sobbing quietly, and put his hand to his face to wipe his eyes. I put my arm around him.

"I always felt a little guilty," he admitted.

"Guilty? It wasn't your fault, Dad. You couldn't do anything about it. You weren't even born yet."

"I know," he said. "I felt guilty that the rest of the family died and I had the chance to live."

"Does Mom know all this?" I asked.

"I tried to explain," he replied. "I guess it's hard to understand unless it happened to your own family."

Dad crumpled up the newspaper and threw it on the floor. Then he stared out the window silently. The farms were gone now. There were buildings out there. Cars. People. We were at the outskirts of Chicago.

"Dad?" I asked after a few minutes had gone by.

"Yeah?"

"Maybe we can do something about it."

"About what?"

"The Holocaust," I said. "We're in 1932. If Adolf Hitler is just running for president of Germany now, that means he hasn't taken power yet. World War II hasn't begun. Maybe we can do something to stop him."

"Don't be silly," Dad said. "What could we possibly do? We're in Chicago, not Germany. Even if we were in Germany, there would be nothing we could do."

"La Salle Street Station!" the conductor suddenly announced. "Chicago, Illinois! Home of the future world champion Chicago Cubs!"

As the train slowed down and pulled into the station, I could see crowds of people standing on the platform. At first, I thought they were waiting to get on the train. But when the train stopped, the people didn't board it. They just stood there.

"We want Babe!" they were chanting. "We want Babe!"

How did they know this was the Yankee train? I wondered. How did everybody always know Babe was there the instant he showed up? As we hustled off the train, Dad said the engineers probably telegraphed ahead to let them know the great Babe Ruth was on board.

Babe could have ignored the chants and hidden in the sleeper car until the crowd broke up. Nobody would have minded. But as soon as he heard the cheering, he poked his head out the window. That only made the crowd cheer louder.

"Does anybody have tickets for Game Five?" Babe bellowed to the crowd out the window.

"Yeah!" a few people answered.

"That's too bad." Babe laughed. "Because there ain't gonna *be* no Game Five! Your Cubbies are gonna lose in four straight! Get the picture?"

He laughed his hearty laugh, and amazingly, so

did the crowd. They didn't seem to care that he was putting down their team. They were just grateful that the great Babe Ruth had spoken to them.

The manager of the Yankees, Joe McCarthy, hustled the team through the crowd. The other players gathered around Babe to shield him from autograph seekers or anyone who might want to harm him. The police held the fans back, but Dad and I managed to follow the Yankees inside the train station.

"Listen!" McCarthy hollered to the team. "Your luggage is being delivered straight to the Edgewater Hotel. You can grab taxis over there. Game time is one-thirty tomorrow. I expect you *all* to be at Wrigley Field by noon for batting practice. No horsing around tonight, or else. Did you hear that, Ruth? None of your guff. *Noon*. That means *you*."

"Yes, sir!" Babe said, giving McCarthy a snappy, exaggerated salute.

The Yankees broke up and scattered in all different directions. We lost sight of Babe immediately.

It was dark out. Dad hailed a cab and we took it to the hotel where the Yankees were staying— the Edgewater. The guy behind the front desk told us the hotel was all booked up because of the World Series, but Dad slipped him a ten-dollar bill and suddenly the guy was able to find a room for us.

The room was nice. I started to complain that it didn't have a TV, but Dad reminded me that television hadn't even been invented yet. I turned on a big radio, though. *The Lone Ranger* was on.

Dad didn't want to hang around the room all night, so we took a walk outside. We found a little coffee shop and had some hamburgers, then Dad got me an ice cream cone to go.

Chicago is on Lake Michigan, and we found ourselves walking along the lake. Dad told me his plan was to get to Wrigley Field during batting practice the next day, so he could scout out the centerfield bleachers and find the best place to catch Ruth's called shot. After the game, we would have to go back home right away because Mom would be waiting.

"Still have our tickets home?" Dad asked as we sat on a bench looking at Lake Michigan.

"Right here," I said, pulling out my unopened pack of baseball cards.

"I'm not that bad a dad, am I, Butch?" he asked suddenly.

"Best one I ever had," I replied, and gave him a punch on the shoulder.

Even though I'd slept a lot on the train from New York, I was still pretty tired, so we went back to the hotel. As I closed my eyes, I was hoping Babe Ruth was getting a good night's sleep. Tomorrow would be one of the biggest days of his life.

And mine.

13

Fathers and Sons

WHEN I WOKE UP THE NEXT MORNING, I COULDN'T HIDE my excitement. The newspaper slipped under the door confirmed it was Saturday, October 1, 1932— the date of the called shot.

"Ready?" Dad asked after he'd showered and dressed.

"Ready as I'll ever be."

We decided to go out and get some breakfast, then head over to Wrigley Field. But as we stepped through the front door of the hotel, somebody tapped me on the shoulder.

"Hey, you boys want to grab some grub? I'm starved."

Dad and I turned around. It was Babe. He had his collar turned up and his hat pulled down over his eyes.

"Uh . . . well . . . "

Dad and I looked at each other. We were hungry, but after what happened in the restaurant Thursday, neither of us really wanted to share another meal with Babe. We just wanted to get him to Wrigley Field in time for the game.

We didn't have to make up an excuse, because a man limped over to Babe and pulled on his sleeve. Babe ignored the guy, and asked us again if we wanted to go out to eat.

"I'm sorry to bother you, Mr. Ruth," the man said, "but my son may be dying."

That got Babe's attention. He looked at the man. The man was wearing an old, tattered gray coat. There were holes in it. He had a sad, sad face, like life had really worn him down.

"My boy's been listening to the games on the radio," the man told Babe. "He's your biggest fan. Can you spare a bat, a ball, an autograph, Babe? Anything from you would mean so much to him."

"Where do you live?" Babe asked.

"In Joliet," the man replied, "about an hour from here."

Babe looked at his watch, then at the man.

"Let's go."

"Where?"

"To Joliet," Babe said. "To see your kid."

"Babe, you don't have time!" Dad protested. "You have to be at Wrigley Field at noon!"

"I'll be there," Babe assured him. "You boys want to tag along?"

"I do!" I said, raising my hand like I was in school.

"You go, Butch," Dad said. "I'll meet you later, in front of the Wrigley Field sign."

"Okay, Dad."

"Come on," Babe said, wrapping his big arms around me and the guy whose son was sick. "Let's hit the road."

Babe dashed into the street, with me and the sick kid's dad right behind. There were no taxicabs waiting at the curb. Babe didn't stand around waiting for one to show up. He just ran into the middle of the street and held up his hand so the next car would have to stop or run him over. A car screeched to a halt just before hitting him. There was a family inside.

"How much you want for your car?" Babe asked the driver.

"Huh?"

"That's Babe Ruth!" a kid in the back seat shrieked.

"Your car," Babe said urgently. "Will you sell it to me for five hundred bucks?"

"Sure!" the driver said happily. He and his family scampered out of the car. Babe peeled off five hundreds from his wallet and gave them to the guy. We piled into the car, Babe in the driver's seat, the sick kid's dad next to him, and me in the back. Babe hit the gas and we roared off, leaving the family standing on the street counting the money.

He pushed the gas pedal to the floor the whole time. He went right through all the lights, whether they were green or red. The rules of the road were for other people. I was sure this was going to be the last day of my life.

"Hang on!" Babe said. Then he started singing "The Sidewalks of New York" again as we screeched down the street.

"Where's the seat belt?" I yelled as Babe careened around the corner, tossing me around like a Ping-Pong ball.

"The what?"

"Forget it," I replied. I guessed they didn't have seat belts in 1932. If we got into an accident in this old tin can, it occurred to me, we would probably all die. The dashboard was made of steel. There were no headrests. Something told me the car was not equipped with antilock brakes or air bags.

The sick kid's dad told Babe what roads he should take to get to the hospital where his kid was staying.

"What's your name?" Babe asked the guy.

"Decker," the guy replied. "Harry Decker."

"Pleased to meetcha, Pop."

Babe turned so he could shake hands with Decker. While they were shaking hands, the car bumped up on a curb and headed straight for a little hot dog stand on the sidewalk.

"Watch out!" I screamed.

Babe swiveled the wheel and missed taking out the hot dog stand by about three inches. The guy selling hot dogs dove out of the way to save his life.

"Nice slide!" Babe roared. "The Cubs oughta sign that guy up!"

Me and Decker failed to see the humor. The hot dog guy had survived Babe's driving. I wasn't sure we would.

" 'East side, west side, all around the town . . .' " Babe sang.

"Slow down!" Decker ordered as Babe gunned the car through the streets of Chicago.

"Can't," Babe hollered back. "Gotta get back to Wrigley Field in time for the game."

"Babe, this is a one-way street!" I screamed.

Cars were veering out of our way left and right to avoid hitting us.

"I'm only goin' one way!" Babe replied with a laugh.

"Watch out for that car!" Decker shouted, putting his hands in front of his eyes.

"What car?" Babe asked.

"The one you nearly slammed into!" I shouted.

A lady was crossing the street about a block ahead of us. She didn't seem to realize how fast Babe was driving and didn't make an effort to hurry.

"Get a load of that sweet patootie!" Babe whistled. "She is one red-hot mama! Hey beautiful!"

"Keep your eyes on the road!" I shrieked as the lady scampered out of the way.

I was sure this was going to be the last day of my life. Just like Babe hit big, missed big, and ate big, he drove big too. He was fearless. He pushed the gas pedal to the floor all the time. He didn't even seem to realize he could tap it gently when he wanted to go slower. He went right through all the lights, whether they were green or red. The rules of the road were for other people, not Babe Ruth. And he just kept on singing, as if he were taking a drive in the country.

"Babe, they're going to take away your driver's license!" I complained after he took a corner so fast the car nearly turned over.

"They can't," he replied. "They took it away five years ago."

Finally we got beyond the city limits. The buildings got smaller, until there were hardly any buildings at all. We were in farm country. Babe was going about seventy miles an hour, but at least we weren't in danger of mowing down pedestrians. I unclenched my fists. My fingernails had made little white lines on the palms of my hands.

That's when we heard the siren.

"!@#$%in' !@#$%!" Babe spat, as he slowed the car down and pulled off to the side of the road. "A cop. Now we're gonna be late."

The police car pulled up behind us, and the officer walked over to the driver's side. He was holding a pad and pen. Babe took off his hat.

"Lemme see your driver's license," he said gruffly.

"Nice day for a drive, huh, officer?" Babe said cheerfully.

The cop looked at Babe and did a double take.

"Y-you're Babe Ruth!" he said, awed.

"Yes, sir!" Babe replied. "Is there something wrong, officer?"

"N-no, Babe," the policeman said, holding out his pad. "Can I have your autograph?"

Babe signed the pad and handed it back. While the officer stared at his autograph, speechless, Babe said good-bye and hit the gas. I turned around to look out the back window as we peeled away. The cop was still staring at the autograph until he was too far away to see anymore.

We got a little lost, but eventually we found the hospital. Instead of looking for a parking place,

Babe just pulled up to the front of the hospital with a screech. There were NO PARKING signs all over.

"Hey!" a guard shouted. "You can't park there, mister!"

"I just did," Babe replied simply.

When the guard realized whom he was speaking to, his mouth dropped open. We all hopped out of the car and the guard rushed to open the door for Babe.

"What's your kid's name?" Babe asked Decker as we approached the information desk.

"Matthew Decker."

"We're here to see Matthew Decker," Babe told the lady behind the desk. Her mouth dropped open, just like the guard's did. She couldn't get any words out, but she did manage to point to a hallway. Babe rushed off in that direction.

Decker found the room his son was in, and he opened the door quietly. The boy was sleeping. He looked like he was around my age or maybe a little older. I couldn't tell what was wrong with him. There were no tubes going into him, and he wasn't hooked up to any machines. But he had bruises on his face and he looked like he was in bad shape. Babe tiptoed to the boy's bedside and pulled up a chair.

"He fell off a horse last week," Decker said softly. "Landed on his head. The doctors aren't sure he's gonna make it."

"I've landed on my head a few times myself," Babe replied, glancing at me.

"Matt," his dad whispered in the boy's ear, "I have a surprise for you."

Babe leaned over Matthew's bed and held the boy's hand. He opened his eyes.

"Hiya, kid!" Babe said.

"Babe Ruth!" he croaked.

"In the flesh, kid. Say, you look like you're a pretty good ballplayer. You rest up good, and pretty soon you'll be outta this joint, ridin' horses again, playin' ball, and havin' fun with your friends."

"Is the World Series over?" Matthew asked.

"We won the first two games," Babe explained. "Game Three is this afternoon. Y'know, kid, I feel hitterish today. Maybe I'll knock a homer for you."

"You will?" Matthew asked. "For me? You promise?"

"I can't promise." Babe chuckled. "But I'll try. I'll make a deal with you. I'll try to hit a homer if you try to get better."

"I *will!*" Matthew exclaimed.

"In that case, I just might hit a couple," Babe said.

A bat, glove, and ball were on the windowsill, along with some of Matthew's other things. Babe went over and picked up the baseball gear.

"It's not polite to go writing on stuff that doesn't belong to you," Babe said, reaching into his jacket, "but I hope you won't mind if I sign my name on these."

"I don't mind," Matthew said happily.

Babe autographed the bat, ball, and glove. Matthew's dad couldn't stop repeating "thank you." I thought Matthew was going to leap out of the bed and start dancing, magically cured.

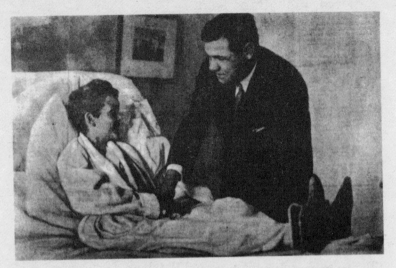

"I'll make a deal with you," Babe told the kid. "I'll try to hit a homer if you try to get better."

"We better get going or I won't be hitting nothin'," Babe told the Deckers.

"Bye, Babe," Matthew said.

"So long, kid."

When we got out into the hallway, Babe leaned heavily against the wall and began to cry. His shoulders bobbed up and down and big tears slid down his cheeks. He pulled a handkerchief out of his pocket and wiped his eyes with it.

"It's okay, Babe," I said, comforting him. "You made him feel better."

"It's not that," Babe said, blowing his nose. "You're so lucky you got a good dad, kid."

"What are you talking about?"

"That guy came all the way to the hotel to get an autograph for his sick kid. Your dad brought you all the way from Kentucky. I never took my little girls anywhere. I've been a lousy father to them. Just like my dad was a lousy father to me."

"I'm sure you're a great father," I assured him. "You love kids. Every boy in the world probably wishes you were his father."

"Signing an autograph for a kid in the hospital and saying good-bye after five minutes is easy," he said sadly. "Being a dad to a kid every day, that's what's so tough."

"Maybe if you spent more time—"

"When I'm with my kids, all I think about is how long until I can eat, drink, play ball, and fool around. It's just the way I am."

As we got back in the car, I realized that I always thought of Babe Ruth as a big, happy hero. Like a cartoon character. But actually he was so much more than that.

He seemed to need so much attention and love that he'd never gotten when he was a kid, but he didn't seem to care what people thought of him. He could be totally thoughtless sometimes and other times incredibly generous. Sometimes he was rough, and other times he was as tender as a puppy. He was happy and outgoing on the outside, but in private he could be sad and emotional. He loved kids, but he couldn't love his own kids. He was like a little immature kid himself.

Babe drove back from the hospital as fast as he'd driven getting there, but more quietly. He didn't sing the whole way. He barely spoke.

"Just be thankful," he said, "you've got a better dad than me."

14

Governor Roosevelt

BY THE TIME BABE AND I GOT BACK TO CHICAGO, IT WAS
one o'clock. The game would be starting in half an
hour. He was late for batting practice. But at least
that old bucket of bolts he was driving hadn't broken down.

Babe seemed to know the streets of Chicago
well. He weaved expertly around the streetcars and
elevated trains. It wasn't long before we were driving up Addison Street and I could see a ballpark
in the distance.

"That's Wrigley Field!" I couldn't help gushing.
Babe looked at me with a what's-the-big-deal look
on his face.

Wrigley Field was one of the few ballparks from
Babe's time that was still standing in my time. I had
never been to Chicago, but Wrigley looked even more
beautiful in 1932 than it looked on TV and pictures in

"That's Wrigley Field!" I gushed. Babe looked at me with a what's-the-big-deal look on his face.

the twenty-first century. Babe pulled the car right up to the front, under a big sign that read:

WRIGLEY FIELD

HOME OF CHICAGO CUBS.

It was a warm, clear, windy day. American flags were whipping in the breeze. Band music was coming from somewhere. Guys were selling peanuts and junky souvenirs. Fans were dashing around trying to round up last-minute tickets, even though signs said TODAY'S GAME SOLD OUT.

In this one spot, at the front of Wrigley Field, it didn't look like there was a Depression. People seemed to have forgotten they had no jobs, no money. Their beloved Cubs were in the World Series. And I knew from reading my baseball books that the Cubs only won the Series two times in the entire twentieth century—in 1907 and 1908.

Lots of people were milling around outside the ballpark. All the men looked the same in their dark jackets, dark pants, and dark hats. I didn't see my dad anywhere.

"It's the Babe!" somebody yelled as Babe and I got out of the car. Instantly, the crowd swarmed toward him.

"I'll see you inside, kid," Babe said, before the crowd enveloped him and swept him into the ballpark.

I wondered where my dad could be. He told me to meet him in front of the Wrigley Field sign before the game. I was sure of that. What if we couldn't find each other? With so many people, I wasn't sure if I could pick him out of the crowd.

My dad had the tickets Babe gave him. If I couldn't find him, I wouldn't be able to get in the ballpark. And if I couldn't get in the ballpark, I couldn't witness the called shot.

Also, if I couldn't find my dad, I realized, he would be stuck in 1932 forever. I was holding the new cards that would take us back home. And he couldn't go back without me anyway.

A newsboy was hawking his papers nearby. "Roosevelt campaigning in Chicago!" he shouted. "Read all about it! New York governor to throw out the first pitch at Game Three today!"

Suddenly I saw Dad through the crowd in the

distance. I recognized him because of the sack of baseballs he was carrying. He saw me, too, and we made our way to each other.

"You okay, Butch?"

"Yeah."

"How's the kid in the hospital?"

"Babe made him feel better," I replied. "Were you able to scope out the centerfield bleachers?"

"Yeah," Dad said. "There are twenty-five rows of seats up there. I know Babe is going to hit the ball to straightaway centerfield and deep. So I'm going to ignore the first ten rows. He probably didn't hit it in the last five rows either, or reporters would have written that he nearly hit the ball out of Wrigley Field. So my hunch is the ball will land around row fifteen. That's where I'm going to be when he hits it."

"Read all about it!" the newsboy shouted again. "New York Governor Franklin Roosevelt in Chicago today to throw out the ceremonial first pitch! See the possible future President of the United States in person!"

Dad whipped his head in the direction of the newsboy. "What did that kid say?" he asked.

"He said Franklin Roosevelt is going to throw out the first pitch of the game," I replied.

Suddenly, Dad had a wild look in his eyes. He fumbled in his pocket for a coin and grabbed a newspaper from the newsboy's stack. Dad read the story on the front page hungrily.

"So what, Dad?"

ROOSEVELT HAILED BY CHICAGO THRONG

200,000 Greet Him on Arrival

MILWAUKEE ENTHUSIASTIC

Governor Makes Plea There to La Follette Followers and Praises Liberalism.

By NED McNENNEY

CHICAGO, Sept. 30. — Franklin D. Roosevelt received from Chicago tonight one of the greatest demonstrations ever accorded a candidate.

With Mayor Cermak at his side he was cheered by tremendous crowds as he rode in an open automobile from the Union Station to the Congress Hotel. The crowd was so dense in places that the motorcycle escort of police had difficulty clearing the way.

Governor Roosevelt is scheduled to throw out the ceremonial first pitch at Wrigley Field today, where the Cubs will take on the New York Yankees in Game Three of the World Series.

"Don't you see, Butch?" my father said excitedly. "Franklin Roosevelt is going to win the election next month. He'll be president of the United States until the end of World War II."

"What does that have to do with us?"

"Remember we saw that article this morning about Hitler running for president of Germany? And I told you about the Holocaust—how Hitler killed all those people, including most of my family?"

"Uh-huh . . ."

"Nobody outside of Germany knew about the Holocaust until the end of the war. If I can get to Roosevelt and tell him what Hitler's going to do . . ."

Dad looked at me. There was fire in his eyes.

"I still don't get it, Dad," I admitted.

"Butch," he said solemnly. "I can stop the Holocaust!"

"Are you serious, Dad?"

"I've got to get to Roosevelt," Dad replied, ignoring my question and marching toward the front gate of Wrigley Field.

"But, Dad," I said, running to keep up with him, "you said it's impossible to change history."

"I've got to *try!*"

He gave me my ticket and handed the ticket taker his stub. We pushed through the turnstile.

"What about catching Babe's called shot?" I asked Dad. "I thought that was so important to you. What about the three million dollars?"

"This is more important, Butch."

I never thought I'd hear my dad say *anything* was more important than money.

Inside the Wrigley Field gate, the smell of popcorn and roasted peanuts hit me. Our seats, Babe had told us, were on the first base side, a few rows behind the Yankee dugout. Dad and I circled the inside of the ballpark until we found the right section.

When the huge green expanse of the outfield came into our view, Dad and I both stopped for a moment and looked at each other with wonder in our eyes.

We were at Wrigley Field, we realized. Not just Wrigley Field, but Wrigley Field in 1932. Not just Wrigley Field in 1932, but Wrigley Field on the day in 1932 when Babe Ruth was going to hit the most famous and controversial homer in baseball history. I had waited a long time for my dad to take me to a big league game. I couldn't have asked for a better one.

"How cool is this?" Dad asked.

"Way cool," I replied.

I had seen Wrigley Field on TV plenty of times. But something was different. It took me a few seconds to figure it out—the famous ivy that covers the outfield walls was missing. The walls were brick. The ivy must not have been planted until after 1932.

Also, there was no ring of lights around the ballpark. Wrigley Field, I remembered, was the last ballpark to have night games. The scoreboard was much smaller, too. I could see there were people sitting inside it, fussing with the big numbers they would put up on the board by hand. On top of the scoreboard were two cute characters that must have been the symbol of Wrigley's gum a long time ago—Doublemint and Spearmint.

Otherwise, the ballpark looked pretty much the same as it would seventy years later. The box seats were close enough to the field that you could hear the players talking. People were sitting with binoculars on the roofs of the buildings across the street, just like they do in the twenty-first century.

Down on the field, the Yankees and Cubs were flipping baseballs back and forth, hitting fungoes, scooping up grounders. I could hardly believe they could catch the ball with those tiny gloves they were wearing.

Dad and I could have just soaked in the atmosphere all day, but he suddenly remembered why he was there and led me to our seats.

"Is Governor Roosevelt here yet?" Dad asked a kid selling cotton candy. The kid shrugged.

We scanned the stands until we spotted a box of seats in the front row on the third base side. There was red, white, and blue bunting hanging over the wall. The seats were empty.

"That must be where Roosevelt will be sitting," Dad said. "He's not here yet."

No sooner had he said that when a buzz spread through the crowd. I looked around to see what had happened.

"Is Roosevelt here?" I asked Dad.

"No," he replied. "Babe is."

Down by the Yankee dugout, Babe had just stepped onto the field. He hadn't hit a homer or done anything spectacular. He just stepped onto the field.

All the people in the ballpark stopped what they were doing to watch. The Cubs stopped playing catch along the foul lines. Even the vendors stopped selling their peanuts to get a good look at the Babe. The only people who didn't stop were the photographers, who were falling all over one another trying to snap Babe's picture. They had these huge cameras, about the size of a wastebasket. When Ruth and Lou Gehrig chatted together for a moment, flashbulbs started popping like the Fourth of July.

When Ruth and Gehrig chatted together for a moment, flashbulbs started popping like the Fourth of July.

In his uniform, Babe looked even bigger than he did in street clothes. Even though he was fat, he moved gracefully. He picked up his bat—bigger and blacker than the others—and whipped it around like a toothpick. Dad had told me that Babe used to call his bat "Big Bertha." He swung so smoothly, so effortlessly. His shoulders must have been incredibly strong.

"Just keep 'em under five runs," Babe shouted to one of the Yankee pitchers. "I'll take care of the rest."

Batting practice was over, but the Babe was the Babe. He stepped up to the plate and one of the Yankees rushed out to the mound to throw him some pitches. The first one bounced in the dirt, but Babe crushed the next one, sending it soaring over the rightfield wall.

"Oooooooooh!" moaned the crowd.

"You ain't seen nothin' yet!" Babe yelled to the Cubs' bench. Then he socked another one over the wall.

"Don't worry about how you guys are gonna get back to New York," Babe hollered, " 'cause we're gonna wrap this thing up right here! You bums are dead meat."

The next pitch came in and Babe took a rip at it, smashing it against the centerfield wall. He missed the next one entirely, and looked at his bat in amazement, as if there must be a hole in it. Then he deposited the next eight pitches in a row over the fence. A few of them sailed out of Wrigley Field. The wind was blowing out toward Lake Michigan, which really made the ball carry.

"I'd play for half my salary if I could hit in this rinky-dink dump all the time!" Babe chuckled, before jogging back to the Yankee dugout.

It was nearly game time, and Roosevelt still hadn't shown up. Maybe he couldn't make it, I thought. Maybe he got stuck in traffic or something. Maybe he changed his mind and decided not to come.

Another buzz went through the crowd, not nearly so loud as the one that greeted Babe. Dad and I scanned the seats until we saw a group of about ten men coming down the third-base side toward the box seats.

"It's Roosevelt!" Dad called, rising from his seat with the sack of baseballs.

I was right behind him as he made his way through the box seats toward the third-base side.

"What are you gonna say to him?" I asked.

"I'm gonna tell him about Hitler," Dad replied. "The gas chambers. The Holocaust. He's got to be told. If Roosevelt had known about the concentration camps, he could have bombed the train tracks feeding into them. I gotta tell him."

Franklin Roosevelt and the men with him worked their way to their seats slowly. I knew that Roosevelt suffered from polio, and those were the days when candidates had to hide a handicap like that from the public. Roosevelt's men, I noticed, were holding him up as they helped him down the steps. To make things harder on the governor, many fans were reaching out to shake his hand.

We were about twenty feet from Roosevelt's box when the Governor reached his seat.

"Governor Roosevelt!" Dad called out. "May I speak with you for a moment, sir?"

The men sitting around Roosevelt turned quickly toward Dad. He climbed over a row of seats so he would be in the same row as the governor. He was about ten seats away.

Four of the men sitting around Roosevelt got up from their seats quickly. Dad climbed past a few people to get closer.

"Governor Roosevelt!" Dad hollered.

Roosevelt turned his head upon hearing Dad's voice. Before Dad could say another word though, one of Roosevelt's men grabbed him roughly around the neck.

"What's in the bag, Bud?" the guy asked.

"Nothin'." Dad grunted. "Hey, get your hands off me!"

"Grab that sack!" screamed one of the other men. "Search him for weapons!"

"I don't have any—" Dad protested, struggling to get free.

"Wait!" I yelled, but nobody heard me.

"Stop him!" somebody yelled.

Three of the guys grabbed Dad, and they started dragging him away.

"Governor Roosevelt!" Dad screamed. "Hitler is going to kill millions of people! You've got to stop him!"

I wasn't sure if Roosevelt heard Dad or not. His

voice was muffled because one of the men had put his hand over Dad's mouth.

"Stop!" I yelled. "Leave him alone!" I began to follow them to see where they were taking my dad.

"Don't, Butch!" Dad hollered to me. "Stay here! See if he calls the shot! I'll find you later! I promise!"

I stopped and watched, like the rest of the crowd, as Dad was handcuffed and forcibly escorted away. There was nothing else I could do.

In a few minutes everything had quieted down, and the fans turned their attention back to the field. A band was marching across the field. Governor Roosevelt stood up and threw out the ceremo-

Governor Roosevelt stood up and threw out the ceremonial first pitch. I made my way back to my seat near the Yankee dugout and sat down to watch the game.

nial first pitch. I made my way back to my seat near the Yankee dugout and sat down to watch the game.

I would be able to see if Babe Ruth called his shot, but I didn't know if I would ever see my dad again.

15

Game Three

WRIGLEY FIELD WAS JAMMED. LOOKING AROUND, I couldn't see an empty seat in the house. That is, except for the seat next to mine. That's where Dad would have been sitting if he hadn't been dragged away by Governor Roosevelt's security guards.

I didn't know where my dad was, what was being done to him, or how we were going to find each other again. I tried to put it out of my mind until the game was over. He promised he would find me later. That was all I had to go on.

An enormous American flag was carried out on the field. It was so large, it couldn't go up any flagpole. Instead, the Cubs and Yankees came out on the infield and held it horizontally. Each player stood about ten feet from the player next to him, being careful not to let the flag touch the ground. Babe was up near the top left corner with the stars.

The flag covered almost the entire infield, like the tarp they use to keep the field dry when it rains.

The crowd was quiet while the marching band played the national anthem. But by the time the umpire announced "Play ball!" the whole crowd was on its feet, roaring. I had to hand it to those Cubs fans—they don't give up. Their team was down two games to none, but it didn't sound like a man, woman, or child in the place had any doubts that their boys would come back.

I knew better. The Cubs were dead. They were going to lose today and lose again tomorrow, and the World Series would be over. The only thing I *didn't* know was whether or not Babe would call his shot. In five innings, though, I would find that out, too.

As the players dashed back into the dugouts, Babe ran past where I was sitting. I waved to him and somehow, in the middle of all those faces calling to him, he noticed mine.

"Hiya, kid!" he yelled to me. "Where's your dad?"

"He . . . had to run an errand," I said.

"A kid your age shouldn't be all by himself. Why don't you come down here and sit with me?"

"Sure!"

The fans around me looked on with awe as I climbed down to the front row and hopped over the rail onto the field. Babe led me into the Yankee dugout.

This was a dream come true. Not only would I

see Babe's called shot, but I was going see it from the best seat in the house! I looked down the Yankee bench. There were Lazzeri, Crosetti, Dickey, Gehrig, and all the others. They were spitting sunflower seeds, pounding their hands into their gloves, giving each other pep talks. It felt like I was in a movie, but I was actually sitting there watching them.

My reverie was interrupted when manager Joe McCarthy stomped over to Babe.

"That kid can't stay in the dugout!" McCarthy thundered, adding a few curse words wherever he could fit one in.

"Oh, yeah?" Babe said calmly. "If the kid can't stay in the dugout, then I'm not stayin' in the dugout, either."

Babe picked up his glove, got up, and went to open the door in the back of the dugout that must have led to the Yankee locker room.

"Sit down, you ugly tub of guts," McCarthy said. "You better wise up!"

When McCarthy stalked away, Babe snickered like a mischievous kid who'd just hit his teacher with a spitball. He helped me into the dugout.

"That guy cramps my style," he giggled.

Babe looked around the field and pointed to the flag in centerfield. "The wind's blowin' out to the right," he said. "If Gehrig and me get the ball up in the air today, we're gonna hit some out of here."

If he only knew what I knew.

The Cubs ran out to take the field for the first

inning. The pitcher, warming up on the side, was a tall right-hander who wore number 12 on the back of his uniform. The public-address announcer introduced him as Charlie Root.

The Cub pitcher was a tall right-hander who wore number 12 on the back of his uniform.

I had seen plenty of games on TV, but I'd never seen a major-league pitcher in person. On TV, a ninety-mile-an-hour fastball never looked that fast to me. It looked like maybe I could even hit it if I got a good swing. But from the Yankee dugout, it looked like Root was firing the ball from a gun. I could barely *see* the ball. And Root was just warming up.

"He ain't got nothin'," Babe said, punctuating the remark with a yawn.

The crowd got louder when Root finished his warm-up pitches. Earle Combs, the first Yankee batter, stepped up to the plate. Joe Sewell went out to the on-deck circle. The fans began yelling and stomping their feet against the bleachers. The noise level grew to a roar as Charlie Root looked in for his sign and let fly the first pitch of the game.

"*Steeeeeerike!*" the umpire hollered as the ball exploded into the catcher's mitt. Game Three was under way. I looked around, just to see if Dad might be on his way back. He wasn't.

Combs looked over a few of Root's pitches, then saw one he liked and smacked a routine grounder toward short. It looked like an easy out, and the fans started clapping.

But the Cub shortstop, Billy Jurges, must have had the jitters. He scooped up the grounder and threw it way over first base.

"Watch out!" Babe hollered. Almost too late, I saw the ball heading right at me in the Yankee dugout. I dove out of the way and it just missed me. When I got up off the floor, Babe and the Yankees were laughing their heads off.

"Welcome to the big leagues, kid!" Babe said, before heading out to the on-deck circle. Tony Lazzeri slid over on the bench so he was sitting next to me. The umpire waved Combs to second base on the overthrow.

Charlie Root wasn't happy about the error. He was stamping around the mound like an angry bull. He walked the next batter, Joe Sewell, on five pitches. That put runners at first and second, nobody out, and it was Babe's turn to hit. The crowd began to hoot and roar.

My dad had told me that Babe was going to hit two homers in Game Three—one in the first inning and then hit his famous called shot in the fifth. So I knew he was about to hit one. I was dying to tell somebody, but I restrained myself.

"Pickle one, Babe!" Bill Dickey shouted as Babe walked slowly to the plate.

If anyone in Wrigley Field didn't know Babe was up, the big number 3 on his back said it loud and clear. He took his time, adjusting his uniform, chatting with the umpire, and drinking in the attention. Babe was a lefthanded pull hitter, and the outfielders shifted around toward rightfield.

Lou Gehrig got out of the dugout and kneeled in the on-deck circle. He wore number 4. The Yankees assigned numbers according to the batting order.

The Chicago Cubs were not impressed that the most famous player in the history of the game was at bat.

"Hey, fatso!" one of the Cubs yelled from the home dugout, "you're all washed up, you balloon-headed meatball!"

"If I had your nose full of nickels, Ruth, I'd be a rich man!"

"Babe, they oughta hitch you to a wagon, you old potbelly!"

Babe laughed. He answered them back, but he wasn't nearly as imaginative as the Cub hecklers. Babe's replies were along the lines of "Oh, yeah?" "Says who?" and "So's your old man!"

Babe stepped into the batter's box and took his stance. He kept his feet close together, so close they were almost touching. His right toe was just a little closer to the plate than his left. He held his bat at the very end; in fact, his pinky finger curled around the knob. As he took a practice swing, he picked up his right foot and glided forward.

Babe didn't swing level, the way Coach Zippel always told us to. His swing was a big uppercut. He didn't lunge or hurry it. It was menacing, but calm and controlled. It was a beautiful thing to watch.

Charlie Root looked in for the sign. The Cubs were heckling Babe, but he didn't notice. He was concentrating on Root's right arm. It looked like a building could collapse right next to him, and he wouldn't notice.

"He's gonna hit one," I mumbled under my breath.

"How do you know?" Lazzeri asked.

"I just know," I replied. "I'm calling his shot."

Root's first pitch was outside. Babe let it go by. Ball one.

His second pitch was inside. Root looked like he was pitching more carefully to Babe than he had to Combs or Sewell. Two balls and no strikes. It was a hitter's count.

"Get it over the plate," one of the Yankees hollered, "you yellow-bellied chowderhead!"

Root started his windup and pumped in the next pitch. It looked like a fastball to me, on the outside corner. Babe brought back his bat slightly and whipped it around so hard he almost fell over. Somehow, he managed to connect.

It looked like a fastball to me. Babe brought back his bat and whipped it around so hard he almost fell over.

The sound of Babe's bat hitting a baseball was different from the sound anyone else's bat made. It was a sharp crack, something like two rocks smacking against each other, hard. The explosion echoed around the stadium.

When the ball left the bat, everyone in the dugout—everyone in the ballpark—rose to their feet to follow its path. This was no line drive. It was a towering moon shot that seemed to hang in the air forever. Babe was almost to second base when the ball finally returned to Earth, deep in the rightfield bleachers.

Gone!

In the dugout, the Yankees jumped up and down, and so did I. They were ahead by three runs, and they hadn't even made an out yet. Babe trotted around the bases in little mincing steps, a smile on his big face. Combs and Sewell were waiting to congratulate him when he got to the plate.

"What a wallop!" Lazzeri marveled.

"Told you he was going to hit one," I said.

"So what?" Lazzeri replied, spitting on the dugout floor. "He hits 'em all the time."

"He's gonna hit another one," I whispered, "in the fifth inning."

It shouldn't have come as a big shock that Babe would hit one out of the park, but the Cub fans sat in their seats, stunned and silent. Babe paused on his way back to the dugout to tip his cap and give a little military salute to the fans. Then he stuck his tongue through his lips and blew a raspberry at them.

"Hey, Charlie, how do you like them apples?" Babe screamed at Root, who was fuming on the mound. "Was that your best fastball? Looked like a change-up to me. I knocked it into the middle of next week! Eat your hearts out, you bums!"

Babe laughed all the way into the Yankee dugout, where the team pounded him on the back.

"Whew!" he exclaimed, wiping his face with a towel as he sat heavily down next to me on the bench. "I'm bushed!"

"From hitting one that hard?" I asked.

"Hitting them is the easy part," Babe replied. "It's running around them bases that wears me out."

While everybody on the bench was laughing, Lou Gehrig walked slowly to the plate. He was different from Babe in just about every way. He was quiet and nervous. He didn't want to be the center of attention. You almost didn't notice he was around.

He was a little shorter than Babe, but more muscular. He didn't have an ounce of fat on him. His thighs were thick and his shoulders wide. His muscles strained against his uniform.

Lou stood closer to the plate than Babe did. He kept his feet much farther apart and took a very short stride. His swing was quick and compact. He didn't corkscrew around the way the Babe did. But it was a more ferocious swing. Gehrig didn't hit high-flying moon shots. He hit line drives that could rip an infielder's glove off his hand.

Not this time, though. Gehrig took a cut at Root's first pitch and grounded out to first base.

*   *   *

The Yankees didn't score any more runs in the first inning. Before the Cubs came to bat, Tony Lazzeri asked me to go get a hot dog for him. I did, and while I was running around the stands looking for a hot dog vendor, the Cubs put a run on the board. The score was 3-1 after one inning.

Babe came to bat again in the second inning and almost hit another one out, but his drive was caught a few feet in front of the centerfield fence. In the third inning, Lou Gehrig got hold of one and drove it over the rightfield wall. That made it 4-1. Then Kiki Cuyler of the Cubs hit a homer, and suddenly the Cubs were back in the game. In the fourth inning, they tied it at 4-4 on a couple of dinky hits and Yankee errors.

But those innings went by in a blur to me. I couldn't concentrate. For one thing, I kept looking around to see if my dad had returned. For another, I knew Babe was going to hit the called shot in the fifth inning, and I kept thinking about it. Also, Tony Lazzeri asked me to get him two more hot dogs, so I spent half the time running around the stands.

When the Yankees got the third Cub out in the fourth inning and trotted into the dugout, my heart began beating faster. Babe would be the second Yankee to bat in the fifth.

It was the moment I had been waiting for.

16

The Called Shot

I STUDIED THE SCOREBOARD CAREFULLY. I WANTED TO make sure I had everything right. It was the top of the fifth inning. Game Three. The score was 4-4. Charlie Root was still on the mound for the Cubs. Joe Sewell was up for the Yankees. Babe went out to the on-deck circle.

Yes, everything was exactly the way Dad told me it would be. Babe was about to hit the most famous home run in baseball history.

The crowd settled down and Root prepared to pitch to Joe Sewell. They played cat and mouse for a few pitches, then Sewell rapped a sharp grounder to short. He was out by a step.

The noise of the crowd increased as Babe approached home plate. It always did. He had booted a ball out in leftfield in the fourth inning and the fans were letting him have it. A single lemon flew out of the stands and bounced near home plate. The boos got louder when the umpire picked up the lemon and tossed it aside.

In the Cub dugout, most of the players were up on the steps, yelling and taunting Babe.

"Drop dead, you big baboon!" one of them hollered.

"Hey, fatso!" yelled another. "When's the last time you saw your feet, you dumb sap?"

"Ah, go soak your heads!" Babe replied. He wasn't angry. He was smiling, even laughing. It looked like he enjoyed being heckled and heckling back.

As Babe stepped into the batter's box, Lou Gehrig climbed out of the dugout and went to kneel in the on-deck circle.

Charlie Root peered in for his sign. He didn't look scared of Babe; he looked determined. Babe had already hit one homer and nearly hit a second one. I almost expected Root to knock Babe down, but instead he burned in a pitch right over the plate. It looked like a fastball. Babe let it go by. When the ump called strike one, the crowd erupted into cheers.

"Fog it in, Charlie!" one of the Cubs yelled. "That big lummox ain't worth a bucket of warm spit."

"Hey, buffalo butt! Is that your mug, Ruth, or were you hit with a really ugly stick?"

The Cubs were having a good time. They were putting their thumbs in their ears and wiggling their fingers at Babe as they shouted at him. They fell all over each other, laughing with each remark.

"Go suck an egg, you bums!" Babe shouted back.

Babe held his bat loosely in his left hand as he stepped out of the batter's box. Still grinning, he looked over at the Cub bench and raised one finger of his right hand in the air. That's one, he was telling them.

When Babe stepped back in, Root threw another pitch, a little slower. It was inside, for ball one.

The next pitch was outside for ball two.

"Booooooo!" screamed the crowd.

Root went into his windup and Babe watched him intently. It looked like he thought about swinging, then changed his mind and let the pitch go by. The umpire called it strike two.

The crowd exploded in cheers. It was deafening. One more strike and they'd have him.

"Time to retire, beer belly! You're finished."

The Cubs were all the way out of their dugout now, trying to scream at Babe over the crowd noise.

Babe stepped out of the box again. He wiped his hands on his pants. Then he held up two fingers on his right hand.

"It only takes one to hit it," he announced, pointing his bat toward the Cub dugout.

"Shut up, you fat blimp!"

This was it. Two balls, two strikes. Two and two. That was the count Dad told me Babe would hit the called shot on. I opened my eyes wide. I didn't want to blink for fear of missing it.

"Hey, kid," Tony Lazzeri said to me, "how about getting me another hot dog?"

"Not *now!*" I barked, not even looking at him.

"Get back in the box, you big galoot," hollered Charlie Root from the mound.

"I'm gonna knock the next pitch down your throat!" Babe replied.

And then he pointed.

It was quick, and you could have missed it if you weren't watching carefully. But he pointed. I was sure of it. Right over Root's head. Straight to centerfield. Babe was holding his bat in his left hand, resting it on his left shoulder. He took his right hand off the bat for an instant and pointed with two fingers of his right hand to centerfield. It was like he was aiming a gun.

"He pointed!" I said to Lazzeri. "Did you see him point?"

"Sit down, kid. You're lucky we let you stay here."

I don't think Root noticed that Babe pointed. He was looking in his glove as he was gripping the ball. Then he looked in for the sign and went into his windup.

Babe didn't choke up on the bat, the way my Little League coaches always told me to when there were two strikes. He held the bat right down at the end as usual.

It was a curve, low and away. Babe lifted his

right leg and took such a big swing that he almost fell down. The crack of the bat could be heard throughout Wrigley Field.

This time, it was a line drive. Babe hit it so low that for an instant I thought the second baseman had a chance to catch it. Then the ball took off, like a golf ball. It started sailing. On the Yankee bench, we all stood up to follow the flight of the ball.

The centerfielder raced back a few steps, but he could tell right away he had no chance. He just stood there watching as the ball sailed far over his head. It disappeared deep into the bleachers, near the flagpole and just below the scoreboard.

The Yankees were screaming with joy. Tony Lazzeri looked at me suspiciously.

Boooooo! screamed the fans.

Almost instantly, stuff started to fly out of the stands and onto the field. Lemons. Tomatoes. Apples. Bananas. People were flinging eggs and cabbages. Somebody tossed an umbrella.

I turned to look at Babe, and he was laughing all the way to first base. He made a remark to the first baseman as he rounded the bag, and he said something to the second baseman, too.

Babe pumped his fist with delight. He pointed to the Cub dugout and thumbed his nose. He was still laughing as he rounded third, laughing so hard he slapped his knee. He held up four fingers and waved them at the Cubs, for four bases, I suppose.

The Chicago dugout looked like a tomb. All the

guys who had been having so much fun heckling Babe sat back on the bench like they had been shot.

I looked over at Franklin Roosevelt's box to see his reaction, but Roosevelt was already gone. He must have caught the first couple of innings and left.

"Did you see that?" I said to the guys on the Yankee bench. "He called his shot! He pointed to centerfield, and then he hit the ball right there!"

"I seen it," Joe Sewell said.

"He did not," insisted Bill Dickey, the Yankee catcher. "He was pointing at Root."

After circling the bases, Babe stepped on home plate ceremoniously and shook hands with Lou Gehrig. Then he bowed to the left, and again to the right. Before he could get into the dugout, the Yankees came out and mauled him.

"You do the same thing," I heard him say to Lou Gehrig.

The umpire had to stop the game for a few minutes so the groundskeepers could pick up all the junk people had thrown onto the field.

People were still buzzing about Babe's homer when Lou Gehrig finally stepped up to the plate. Some of them didn't even notice that Gehrig swung at Charlie Root's first pitch and drove it over the rightfield wall. The back-to-back Yankee homers made the score 6-4.

The Cubs were beaten. You could see it in their eyes. They didn't have anything else to say. Ruth and Gehrig had each slammed two home runs, and

Babe shook hands with Lou Gehrig after crossing the plate and told him, "You do the same thing."

Chicago simply couldn't match that kind of fire-power. The game might as well have been over.

So I had seen it. To my eyes, at least, Babe had called his shot. I had accomplished what I'd set out to do. But now I had to do something else—find my dad.

17

Something Better

I DIDN'T STICK AROUND TO SEE THE END OF THE GAME. After the sixth inning, I left the Yankee dugout and hopped over the wall into the stands. The Cub fans were sitting there in their seats stunned, like a boxer who had just been pummeled.

I asked myself this question—*How am I going to find my father in a crowd of fifty thousand people . . . and a city of millions?*

I had to do some serious thinking. The last time I saw Dad, the game was about to begin and some guys were dragging him away because they thought he was threatening the life of Franklin Roosevelt. He could be anywhere.

Maybe he was in jail. Maybe they were questioning him as if he was John Wilkes Booth or something. Maybe he had escaped on the way to jail. Maybe there was a manhunt. Maybe they shot him. Maybe—

I was being ridiculous.

There was no point in trying to find Dad in the stands. If he was in Wrigley Field, I reasoned, he would simply go to our seats and find *me*. Our seats were empty, so Dad had to be outside the ballpark.

I could go to one of the Yankee officials and see if someone could help track Dad down, I thought as I made my way toward the exit. Maybe they could make an announcement over the public-address system—"We have a lost child in section fifty-four."

Nah. When I reached Addison Street in front of Wrigley Field, the thought crossed my mind that maybe I should do nothing. I mean, until a few days ago, what had my dad ever done for *me?* Not much. I could just go find a quiet grassy spot by myself and use my new baseball cards to take me back home. I could just leave Dad in 1932 and let him fend for himself.

But that would be wrong, I decided. And besides, being together for the last couple of days had brought us closer together. I wanted him to be part of my life when I got back home.

If I was my dad, where would I be? I wondered.

At that moment, everything went black. Somebody had slapped two big hands over my eyes from behind and gripped my head tight. I struggled to turn my head around but the hands held me firm.

"Guess who?" the voice asked.

"Dad!"

I whirled around, and we grabbed each other in a big bear hug.

"So," Dad said. "Did he point? Did Babe call his shot or not?"

"I think so."

"You *think* so?"

"Well, it looked to me like he called his shot," I explained, "but some of the guys on the bench said he was just pointing and yelling at the pitcher."

"The guys on the bench?" Dad asked, amused.

"Yeah," I said, "I was watching from the Yankee dugout."

Dad shook his head and laughed. "I think our luck is changing, Butch," he said.

I noticed he had a slightly blackened eye and his jacket was torn.

"Are you okay, Dad?"

"They roughed me up a little dragging me out of the ballpark," he replied, "but I'll be all right."

"So you never delivered the message to Roosevelt?"

"No," Dad said. "But I tried. At least I made the effort. And somehow, I feel good about that."

"Did they put you in jail or anything?"

"Nah. They took me to a police station and questioned me for a few minutes. When they saw that I wasn't nuts and that all I had in the sack was a bunch of baseballs, they let me go."

The sack! I had forgotten about it! Dad wasn't holding the sack filled with baseballs autographed by Babe Ruth!

"Where is it?" I asked, concerned.

"They confiscated it," Dad said simply. He had a little smile on his face, like he had a secret to share with me.

"You don't look very upset," I pointed out.

"I'm not," Dad said, as he reached into his jacket pocket. "I've got something better."

He gently pulled out a baseball with two fingers and held it up for me to see, like he was holding a rare coin. The ball was clean and white, with one smudge mark on it. It wasn't autographed or anything.

"A baseball?" I asked, puzzled. "I don't get it."

"Not just any baseball," Dad teased, continuing to smile slyly at me.

Slowly, gradually, I came to appreciate the significance of what Dad was holding before my eyes.

"You *caught* it?" I shouted, my mouth and eyes open as wide as they could possibly be. "You caught Babe Ruth's called shot?"

"Well, not exactly," Dad said modestly. "You see, after the cops let me go, I went back to the ballpark. Roosevelt was gone, so I went to the centerfield stands, where I knew the ball was going to land. I was a couple of rows away when it came down. It bounced off some lady's head and rolled under some seats. Me and a few other guys dove for it, but I got there first. They tried to beat it out of me. That's how I got the black eye, actually. But I wouldn't let 'em have the ball."

I took the ball in my hand and examined it. It

looked like any other baseball I'd seen, but holding this one made me tremble. Not only had I seen Babe Ruth hit the most famous home run in baseball history, but now the ball he hit was in my hand.

It doesn't get much better than this, I thought to myself.

"I want you to have it," Dad said, smiling at me.

"To keep?" I asked, astonished.

"To keep," he said. "Being with you these last few days was good enough for me. Just having the chance to do something about the Holocaust gives me a peace of mind I've never felt. This is my present to you."

He took the ball in his hand again and looked at it for a moment. Then he nodded his head and gave it to me.

"What about the money?" I asked. "It could be worth three million bucks."

"What am I gonna do with three million bucks?" Dad asked. "I'd just give it to you as an inheritance someday anyway."

Dad and I hugged each other again.

After we finished pretending that neither one of us was crying, we both realized something—the called shot ball wasn't worth a dime unless we had Babe Ruth sign it, date it, and write on it exactly what inning he hit it.

We had promised Babe that we wouldn't ask him to sign anything else, but I figured he wouldn't mind writing his name on just one more baseball. Especially a baseball that he'd hit for a game-winning home run in the World Series.

Dad and I rushed back inside Wrigley Field. The stands were mostly empty now, except for a few depressed Cub fans still sitting there like they were at a funeral. We hopped over the rail and into the Yankee dugout. The door in the back of the dugout led to the locker room.

Most of the players were still there, changing into their street clothes and happily discussing the game. I didn't see Babe anywhere.

An equipment manager was shoving bats and gloves and catcher's gear into a big canvas bag.

"Where's Ruth?" Dad asked him. "My son wants him to sign a ball."

"The big ape already left." The equipment manager laughed. "Off to some party at Al Capone's house, I heard."

"But we've got the home-run ball!" Dad said urgently. "I caught the ball that Babe hit in the fifth inning."

"You and everybody else." The equipment manager chuckled. "Just throw it in that bucket with the others."

In front of Babe's locker was a metal bucket filled to the brim with baseballs.

"But our ball is the real one!" I protested.

"Sure, sonny," the guy said. "Just toss it in the bucket and come back tomorrow around dinner time. I'll ask Babe if he'll sign 'em all."

"We can't come back tomorrow!"

The guy shrugged. Dad put his arm around my shoulder.

"Let's go home now, Butch."

18

Slipping Away

DAD AND I WALKED OUT OF WRIGLEY FIELD ALMOST IN A daze. I flipped the baseball Dad had given me up in the air and caught it. There would be no way to prove it was the ball Babe hit for his famous called-shot home run. When I got back home, it would just be an ordinary baseball. I wouldn't be able to sell it for ten dollars, much less three million.

But I wasn't too depressed. Seeing Babe Ruth hit the homer had been all I'd wanted in the first place. And, as a bonus, Dad and I had gotten to know Babe—and each other.

"How do we do it, Butch?" Dad asked as we crossed Waveland Avenue outside the ballpark. "How do we get back home?"

"Are you sure you want to go back?" I asked him. "Movies are only fifty cents here, y'know. Breakfast is a quarter. You can live pretty well in 1932."

"I'm sure," Dad said, throwing an arm over my shoulder.

"We've got to find a nice, quiet place."

Down the street was a big vacant lot. Dad and I headed for it. There was no grass on the ground. Just dirt, with weeds popping up through the cracks here and there. There was some garbage strewn about. Dad and I sat down against the wall of the building at the edge of the lot, being careful not to sit on any broken glass or sharp objects. A group of boys was playing ball at the other end of the lot, but they were too far away to bother us.

I took my pack of new baseball cards out of my pocket. They would be our airline tickets home. I handed the pack to Dad to open. I flipped the Ruth baseball in the air.

"I thought you told me you couldn't travel through time with recent cards," Dad said.

"I can't," I explained. "But in 1932, these aren't recent cards. They're cards from seventy years into the future. They should be very powerful."

Dad tore off the plastic wrapper and fingered the cards.

"Last chance to change your mind, Dad."

"No," he said. "I want to go with you."

"What are you going to do when we get home?" I asked.

"Get a job," Dad said right away. "It should be a lot easier than it is here."

"I'm sorry you didn't make a lot of money here."

"That's okay," he replied. "I got something better."

I took his hand, the same way I did back on the living room couch a few days earlier. Before closing our eyes, we looked around to take one last glimpse at 1932.

The boys at the other end of the lot were in the middle of a pickup game. I could see there were runners on second and third base, which were simply pieces of old roof shingle. The bat they were using looked like the handle of a broken axe. None of them had a baseball glove or any protective gear. The catcher was using an old pillow to cushion his hand. These were poor kids, Depression kids.

The pitcher went into his windup and whipped a pitch over the plate. The batter swung the big axe handle and connected. It was a long drive, over the head of the rightfielder, toward where Dad and I were sitting. The rightfielder started chasing it, but the ball took a big hop off the hard dirt and barely slowed down at all. The runners scored easily, and the kid who hit the ball tore around the bases for an inside-the-park home run.

The ball kept rolling, until it stopped about fifteen feet in front of us.

"Hey kid!" the rightfielder shouted to me, panting for breath. "How about a little help?"

I stood up and picked up the ball. It was a ratty old thing, torn, lumpy, and discolored. It looked like it had been made from an old sock with a rock inside, probably wrapped with tape or yarn.

I held the lumpy ball in my left hand and the called-shot ball in my right hand. I was about to throw back the kid's ball, but I stopped.

I looked over at Dad. He nodded his head slightly, a small smile on his face. He was thinking the same thing I was thinking.

I stuck the ratty old ball in my pocket and threw the kid the Ruth ball.

The kid caught my throw on one hop. He was about to whirl around and wing the ball back to his friends, but he stopped and looked at what he had in his hand. I saw him flinch. Then he looked at the ball carefully, gripping it different ways. A big smile spread across his face. He'd probably never held a real baseball in his hands, it occurred to me.

"Whaddaya waitin' for, ya dope?" one of the others shouted. "Throw it in!"

The kid looked at me and waved, then dashed toward the infield to show the ball to his friends. They huddled around him and looked at it like he had discovered buried treasure.

"Ready, Dad?"

"Ready."

He handed me a card from the pack. I didn't even notice what player was on it. It didn't matter. I closed my eyes and held Dad's hand with one hand and the baseball card with the other. I thought about what it would be like to be home. To be back in my own time. My own house. With my own stuff.

The tingling sensation began almost immediately. That buzzy feeling moved up my fingertips, through my arms, and across my body.

I began to feel myself slipping away.

19

Attack!

A WEEK LATER . . . COACH ZIPPEL BENT DOWN AND PLUCKED a few blades of grass from the area behind the Yellow Jackets bench at Dunn Field. He tossed them in the air and watched them blow away.

"The wind's blowing out, everybody," he informed us.

Our game was about to begin. The parents on the sidelines were pulling out toys and snacks to keep their babies and toddlers occupied while we played.

I stole a peek at the batting order on the clipboard Coach Zippel was holding. He had moved me up to second in the lineup, which made me feel good. The number two batter is supposed to be a kid who can consistently get the bat on the ball and advance the runner. I had been swinging the bat really good—I mean *well*. I was feeling kind of, oh . . . hitterish.

We were playing the University Orthopedic Surgeons, who had beaten us earlier in the season. They jumped out to a quick 2-0 lead in the first inning, but we tied it in the second. We scored two more runs in the fourth inning, but they came back with two in the fifth. The score was tied at 4-4.

I hit the ball pretty hard my first three times up, but each time I hit it right at somebody. The third one was a bullet that would have hit the first baseman in her face if she hadn't stuck up her hand in self-defense. When she looked in her glove, she was astonished to find the ball there. I was robbed of a sure double.

The game was still tied after six innings. Ordinarily, six innings is all we play in our league. But if the score is tied at the end of six, we're allowed to play an extra inning—as long as the seventh inning doesn't start more than two hours after the game began. Those are league rules.

The sun was starting to set. The umpire told both coaches he would have to call the game in fifteen minutes on account of darkness. They're always worried that some kid might not see the ball in the dark and get hurt.

Coach Zippel whispered to our pitcher, Casey Tyler, to throw the ball over the plate and try to make the Surgeons hit it. The faster we could get them out, the sooner we would get our turn at bat. We rushed out on the field, and I took my position at third base.

Fortunately, the first two Surgeons both swung

at Casey's first pitches. One of them hit a pop-up to me at third, and the other grounded out to second. Two outs. Their next batter struck out on four pitches.

We dashed to our bench. We had ten minutes, tops, to score a run and win the game. Otherwise, it would go in the books as a tie. I grabbed a batting helmet and my batting gloves. I would be up second.

"Go up there swinging, kids," Coach Zippel instructed us. "We've got to score a run *now*."

Kevin Dougrey led off for us. He swung at the first pitch, too, and hit a dinky grounder to third. It should have been an easy out, but the third baseman didn't get his glove down and the ball glanced off the webbing. Kevin was safe at first.

"Nice hit, Kev!" Kevin's mom shouted from the "mom" section of the bleachers. Mrs. Dougrey was clueless about baseball. She doesn't realize it's no great achievement to reach first base on an error.

But at least we had a base runner. I picked out my favorite bat and hustled up to the plate. I didn't want the ump to stop the game in the middle of my at bat.

"Whack it, Joey!"

I could tell from the sound of the voice that it was my mom. I scanned the leftfield foul line to check the "mom" section. She wasn't there. I spotted her sitting closer to home plate. That was odd. She gave me a little wave and gestured with her hand to her right.

I looked to the right of Mom. Sitting next to Mom was . . .

Dad!

Huh?

I stepped out of the batter's box and asked the umpire for time out. Dad had never come to one of my Little League games before. I shook my head to make sure I wasn't seeing things. It was Dad all right. He flashed me a thumbs-up.

"Let's go, Joe!" hollered Coach Zippel. "He's gonna stop the game any minute."

"Are you okay, son?" the umpire asked.

"Yeah," I said, getting back into the batter's box. Thoughts were flying through my mind. What was my dad doing here? Were Mom and Dad getting back together again? Or were they just sitting together to make me feel good? I tried to put it all out of my mind and focus on the pitcher.

"Smash it, Stoshack!" one of my teammates yelled from the bench.

"Five minutes, coaches!" yelled the umpire. "It's getting dark out here."

"No batter, no batter," one of the Orthopedic Surgeons hollered.

I looked over to Coach Zippel. He touched the brim of his cap with his left hand. That's our bunt sign.

Bunt?

That took me by surprise. The last time I bunted, the coach told me I'd made a big mistake. He told me what a good hitter I was and said I should have swung away. Now he was telling me to lay down a *bunt?* It didn't make sense.

I looked over at Coach Zippel again just to make sure I had the sign right. He touched the brim of his cap with his left hand again. Yeah, he wanted me to bunt.

I thought about the situation. Kevin was on first base with nobody out. Casey Tyler would be coming to bat after me, and he was the best hitter on our team. If I laid down a quick bunt and advanced Kevin to second base, he would be able to score on a single by Casey. But if I got a single, Kevin wouldn't be able to score all the way from first. He would only make it to third, and the umpire could stop the game at any time.

I had to admit Coach Zippel's strategy made a certain amount of sense.

I set my feet in the batter's box. The pitcher looked in for his sign. As he went into his windup, I squared around to bunt.

The pitch came in. It was perfect, right down the heart of the plate. When you're swinging the bat well, the ball looks bigger and slower, for some reason. It looked like a big, fat melon floating up to me in slow motion. Or an ice cream sundae. With marshmallow sauce.

What a shame it would be to waste such a juicy pitch on a dinky little bunt.

Attack the ball! That's what Coach Zippel always tells us when we have batting practice. *Pretend the ball is your worst enemy. The schoolyard bully. That cousin you hate. This is your chance to teach them a lesson. Attack!*

I couldn't resist. I attacked.

I brought my bat back far and whipped it through the strike zone as hard as I could. I swung so hard that I almost fell down.

Somehow, I made contact, and it felt *good*.

Sometimes when I hit the ball, the vibration from the bat stings my hands. There was no sting this time. I hit it right on the sweet spot. The ball took off toward rightfield.

At first I didn't think it had much distance. But then the ball got up into the wind and it carried. I took off for first.

Nobody has ever hit a ball out of Dunn Field. When I saw the rightfielder backpedaling, I knew I had a chance.

"Go!" my teammates were shouting. "Go!"

The rightfielder had his back against the fence. The ball was over his head. It made it over the Moyer Dry Cleaning sign. Over the Karjane Hardware sign. Over the Biros Used Cars sign at the top of the fence.

Then it sailed out of Dunn Field and everybody went nuts.

There was a bang in the parking lot behind the field. A bunch of little brothers and sisters went running off to retrieve the ball.

They can never say that nobody ever hit a ball out of Dunn Field again, I thought, *because I just did.*

I slapped hands with the first-base coach. The kid playing shortstop for the other team didn't shake my hand or anything, but he did say "Nice smack!" when I jogged past. Then I high-fived our third-base coach. The Yellow Jackets mobbed me when I jumped on home plate with both feet.

"Okay, let's call it a game," the umpire announced.

My heart was pumping so fast and I was on such a high that I couldn't think straight. Everybody was shouting and pounding me on the back and taking pictures of me. The little girl who'd retrieved the ball came over with a pen and actually asked me to sign it for her.

I saw Dad coming down from the bleachers to congratulate me, but Coach Zippel got to me first. He put his arm around my shoulder.

"Boy, you bunt *hard*," he said.

"I'm sorry, Coach," I replied. "The pitch was coming in like a big lollipop and I just couldn't resist taking a cut at it."

"It's okay, Joe," the coach said. "It worked out for the best. Who taught you to swing like that?"

I wasn't sure what to say. My dad was next to us now, and I was a little tongue-tied. I still couldn't get over the fact that he'd showed up for the game.

"Must've been Babe Ruth," Dad said, squeezing my shoulder.

Everybody laughed, but Dad and I knew the truth.

To the Reader

EVERYTHING YOU READ IN THIS BOOK WAS TRUE, EXCEPT—
of course—for the stuff I made up. It's only fair to
tell you which was which.

Joe Stoshack and his dad are fictional characters, and there's no evidence that time travel is
possible. (Too bad, huh?) But most of the events
described in 1932 were real.

Franklin Roosevelt *did* throw out the first pitch
at the "called-shot game" on October 1, 1932. Five
weeks later he was elected President of the United
States. Coincidentally, just nineteen days after
Roosevelt took the oath of office, Adolf Hitler became the dictator of Germany.

Each of these very different men led his nation
for twelve years. To pile coincidence on top of coincidence, they died within three weeks of each other

in 1945—Roosevelt of a cerebral hemorrhage and Hitler by suicide.

While President Roosevelt and the Allies were aware that the Nazis were committing atrocities, nobody knew the full extent of the Holocaust until German concentration camps were liberated at the end of World War II.

I tried to paint an accurate picture of the Depression in this book. To give you an idea of how tough times were in America, consider the following statistics for 1932: One out of every four men was unemployed. The people who did have jobs earned an average of $17 a week. Thirty-four million Americans had no income at all. Twenty thousand businesses went bankrupt that year, and 1,616 banks failed. Twenty-one thousand people committed suicide.

Even the great Babe Ruth suffered in the Depression, seeing his salary drop all the way from a then-enormous $80,000 a year to $35,000 when he left baseball in 1935.

To describe the Babe's personality, I read many biographies of the man. Most helpful were *Babe Ruth's America* by Robert Smith, *Babe Ruth and the American Dream* by Ken Sobol, *Babe: The Legend Comes to Life* by Robert Creamer, *Babe Ruth: His Life and Legend* by Kal Wagenheim, and *The Life That Ruth Built* by Marshall Smelser.

I tried to show that Babe was a complicated man—fun-loving yet sad, impulsive but generous, immature and incredibly talented all at the same time. Babe's appetite and poor driving skills are exaggerated in this story, but only slightly. He will, in all likelihood, always be the most famous baseball player in history.

Babe began getting painful headaches in November of 1946 and he was diagnosed with rare nasopharyngeal cancer. He was just fifty-three years old when he died on August 16, 1948. He is buried in Gate of Heaven Cemetery in Hawthorne, New York.

Did He Point?

The question of whether or not Babe Ruth truly called his shot in Game Three of the 1932 World Series can only be answered if we do someday figure out a way to travel through time. Even eyewitnesses to the event disagreed. But, for the record, here is what they had to say about it.

"What do you think of the nerve of that big monkey, calling his shot and getting away with it?"
—Lou Gehrig, Yankee first baseman and on-deck batter

"Ruth pointed with his bat in his right hand, to rightfield, not centerfield. But he definitely called his shot."
—Lefty Gomez, Yankee pitcher

"He was pointing at Root, not at the centerfield stands."
—Bill Dickey, Yankee catcher

"Yes, he pointed to the fence. Ruth, after two strikes, got out of the batter's box, dried his hands off, got back in the box with his bat in his left hand, and two fingers of his right hand pointed in the direction of centerfield, looking at the Cubs bench all the time."
—Joe Sewell, Yankee third baseman

"Ruth pointed toward the centerfield fence, but he was pointing at the pitcher."
—Ben Chapman, Yankee rightfielder

"Before taking his stance he swept his left arm full length and pointed to the centerfield fence."
—Doc Painter, Yankee trainer

"I'm not going to say he didn't do it. Maybe I didn't see it. Maybe I was looking the other way."
—Joe McCarthy, Yankee manager

"Babe Ruth did not call his home run."
—Woody English, Cub third baseman

"Ruth did point, sure. He definitely raised his right arm. He indicated where he'd already hit a home run. But as far as pointing to center, no he didn't. You know darn well a guy with two strikes isn't going to say he's going to hit a home run on the next pitch."
—Mark Koenig, Cub shortstop

"He didn't point, don't kid yourself. If he pointed, do you think Root would have thrown him a strike to hit?"
—Billy Herman, Cub second baseman

"I hesitate to spoil a good story, but the Babe actually was pointing to the mound."
—Charlie Grimm, Cub first baseman

"Ruth did not point at the fence before he swung. If he had made a gesture like that, well, anybody who knows me knows that Ruth would have ended up on his ____."
—Charlie Root, Cub pitcher

"Of course I didn't see him point. Nobody else saw him point, because he didn't. Charlie would have thrown it right at his head."
—Dorothy Root, Charlie Root's wife

"If he had pointed out at the bleachers, I'd be the first one to say so."
—Gabby Hartnett, Cub catcher

"Don't let anybody tell you different. Babe definitely pointed."
—Pat Pieper, broadcaster

"Sure he called the shot. No doubt about it."
—Robert Creamer, author of *Babe: The Legend Comes to Life*

"He pointed in the direction of dead centerfield."
—Tom Meany, author of *Babe Ruth*

"Where he pointed is a subject of debate."
—Kal Wagenheim, author of *Babe Ruth: His Life and Legend*

"A single lemon rolled to the plate as Ruth came up in the fifth and in no mistaken motions, the Babe notified the crowd that the nature of his retaliation would be a wallop right out of the confines of the park."
—John Drebinger, *The New York Times*

"RUTH CALLS SHOT AS HE PUTS HOMER NO. 2 IN SIDE POCKET."
—*New York World Telegram*, October 1, 1932

"He pointed like a duellist to the spot where he expected to send his rapier home."
—Paul Gallico, *New York Daily News*, October 3, 1932

"He called his shot theatrically, with derisive gestures towards the Cubs dugout."
—*San Francisco Examiner*, October 2, 1932

"Why don't you read the papers? It's all right there in the papers."
—Babe Ruth

BABE RUTH'S CAREER STATISTICS

BATTING RECORD

YEAR	GAMES	AT BATS	RUNS	HITS	DOUBLES	TRIPLES	HOME RUNS	RUNS BATTED IN	STOLEN BASES	BATTING AVERAGE	SLUGGING AVERAGE
BOSTON RED SOX											
1914	5	10	1	2	1	0	0	0	0	.200	.300
1915	42	92	16	29	10	1	4	21	0	.315	.576
1916	67	136	18	37	5	3	3	16	0	.272	.419
1917	52	123	14	40	6	3	2	12	0	.325	.472
1918	95	317	50	95	26	11	11*	66	6	.300	.555*
1919	130	432	103*	139	34	12	29*	114*	7	.322	.657*
NEW YORK YANKEES											
1920	142	458	158*	172	36	9	54*	137*	14	.376	.847*
1921	152	540	177*	204	44	16	59*	171*	17	.378	.846*
1922	110	406	94	128	24	8	35	99	2	.315	.672*
1923	152	522	151*	205	45	13	41*	131*	17	.393	.764*
1924	153	529	143*	200	39	7	46*	121	9	.378*	.739*
1925	98	359	61	104	12	2	25	66	2	.290	.543
1926	152	495	139*	184	30	5	47*	145*	11	.372	.737*
1927	151	540	158*	192	29	8	60*	164	7	.356	.772*
1928	154*	536	163*	173	29	8	54*	142*	4	.323	.709*
1929	135	499	121	172	26	6	46*	154	5	.345	.697*
1930	145	518	150	186	28	9	49*	153	10	.359	.732
1931	145	534	149	199	31	3	46*	163	5	.373	.700*
1932	133	457	120	156	13	5	41	137	2	.341	.661
1933	137	459	97	138	21	3	34	103	4	.301	.582
1934	125	365	78	105	17	4	22	84	1	.288	.537
BOSTON BRAVES											
1935	28	72	13	13	0	0	6	12	0	.181	.431
22 years	2503	8399	2174	2873	506	136	714	2211	123	.342	.690

*Led League

WORLD SERIES

YEAR	GAMES	AT BATS	RUNS	HITS	DOUBLES	TRIPLES	HOME RUNS	RUNS BATTED IN	STOLEN BASES	BATTING AVERAGE	SLUGGING AVERAGE
BOSTON RED SOX											
1915	1	1	0	0	0	0	0	0	0	.000	.000
1916	1	5	0	0	0	0	0	1	0	.000	.000
1918	3	5	0	1	0	1	0	2	0	.200	.600
NEW YORK YANKEES											
1921	6	16	3	5	0	0	1	4	2	.313	.500
1922	5	17	1	2	1	0	0	1	0	.118	.176
1923	6	19	8	7	1	1	3	3	0	.368	1.000
1926	7	20	6	6	0	0	4	5	1	.300	.900
1927	4	15	4	6	0	0	2	7	1	.400	.800
1928	4	16	9	10	3	0	3	4	0	.625	1.375
1932	4	15	6	5	0	0	2	6	0	.333	.733
							15			.326	.744

PITCHING RECORD

	YEAR	GAMES	INNINGS PITCHED	WON	LOST	WINNING PERCENTAGE	BASES ON BALLS	STRIKEOUTS	HITS	SHUTOUTS	EARNED RUN AVERAGE
BOSTON RED SOX	1914	4	23	2	1	.667	7	3	21	0	3.91
	1915	32	217.2	18	8	.692	85	112	166	1	2.44
	1916	44	323.2	23	12	.657	118	170	230	9*	1.75*
	1917	41	326.1	24	13	.649	108	128	244	6	2.01
	1918	20	166.1	13	7	.650	49	40	125	1	2.22
	1919	17	133.1	9	5	.643	58	30	148	0	2.97
NEW YORK YANKEES	1920	1	4	1	0	1.000	2	0	3	0	4.50
	1921	2	9	2	0	1.000	9	2	14	0	9.00
	1930	1	9	1	0	1.000	2	3	11	0	3.00
	1933	1	9	1	0	1.000	3	0	12	0	5.00
	10 years	163	1221.1	94	46	.671	441	488	974	17	2.28

*Led League

	YEAR	GAMES	INNINGS PITCHED	WON	LOST	WINNING PERCENTAGE	BASES ON BALLS	STRIKEOUTS	HITS	SHUTOUTS	EARNED RUN AVERAGE
WORLD SERIES											
BOSTON RED SOX	1916	1	14	1	0	1.000	3	4	6	0	0.64
	1918	2	17	2	0	1.000	7	4	13	1	1.06
	2 years	3	31	3	0	1.000	10	8	19	1	0.87

Permissions

The author would like to acknowledge the following for use of photographs and artwork:

"The Called Shot" by Matt Kandle, copyright © 1990 by Kirk Kandle, all rights reserved: 2; Nina Wallace: 25, 27, 39, 87, 109; Library of Congress: 31, 51; National Baseball Hall of Fame Library, Cooperstown, N.Y.: 36, 56, 75, 81, 96, 106; Babe Ruth Birthplace and Baseball Center: 38, 102, 126; National Archives: 113; Franklin D. Roosevelt Library: 117; Brace Photos: 122; Associated Press/ Wide World Photos: 136.